Christin Lore Weber

ALSO BY CHRISTIN LORE WEBER

ALTAR MUSIC

GYPSY BONES

THE FARNEAR JOURNALS

THE BLUE SHAWL

THE EDGE OF TENDERNESS

THE ROOT OF BEAUTY

CIRCLE OF MYSTERIES

FINDING STONE

A CRY IN THE DESERT

BLESSINGS

WOMANCHRIST

CARING COMMUNITY

WIDOW'S WALK

Christin Lore Weber

LEAVING

She woke the morning with her preparations,
Sweeping the clutter from the door
Leaves piled there by wind
A disturbance in the night
Like mice scurrying in.

She had thought to stay,
Her affection for her house compelling her
To hold onto it with feathers saved
From the birds of summertime
And stones gathered from the creek
Some of them gold.

But there had come signs,
A shower of meteors above the mountain
Followed by green veils, light waving from the north
Reaching downwards from infinity
And she had raised her hand to hold
What never could be held.

It was deep winter when she finally left,
Her door open to the wind and whatever else
Might seek shelter there
As snow dusted the paths
And covered the remains of her presence
On that winding way.

WIDOW'S WALK

CHRISTIN LORE WEBER

CYBERSCRIBE PUBLICATIONS

5

Christin Lore Weber

CyberScribe Publications
Casa Chiara Hermitage
9700 Sterling Creek Road, Jacksonville, 97530

ISBN 978-0-9835500-5-1

COVER ART

I Have Always Been With You
2015 Acrylic on Canvas Painting by Shiloh Sophia
www.shilohsophia.com

Widow's Walk

FOR THE STRANGER

Christin Lore Weber

WIDOW'S WALK

MYSTERY IS A GREAT EMBARRASSMENT FOR THE
MODERN MIND.

-FLANNERY O'CONNOR

WISDOM IS BRILLIANT, SHE NEVER FADES.
BY THOSE WHO LOVE HER, SHE IS READILY SEEN
BY THOSE WHO SEEK HER, SHE IS READILY FOUND,
...
FOR SHE HERSELF SEARCHES EVERYWHERE
FOR THOSE WHO ARE WORTHY OF HER,
BENEVOLENTLY APPEARING TO THEM
ON THEIR WAYS.

-WISDOM 6:12,16

Christin Lore Weber

The Prairie Region

News from Greenleaf, Common Place, and
Surrounding Townships

May 18, 1977

Obituaries

WILLIAM PAUL FENELON
Born: March 21, 1942—Died: May 17, 1977

The sudden death of William (Will) Fenelon stunned the residents of Common Place of which he was a lifelong resident. His grandfather, Stephen Fenelon, homesteaded what is now the Paul Fenelon Ranch where Will was born thirty-five years ago. He attended school at the Common Place Grade School and then at the high school in Greenleaf. After graduation in 1960 he married Beatrice Breault whose father owned the property adjacent to the Fenelon Ranch. On that land Will and Beatrice produced the largest alfalfa crop in the region. Will is survived by his wife, Beatrice, and his father Paul Fenelon.

A Memorial will be held outside the Common Place Bible Church on Saturday, May 21, at 11:00 A.M.

THE STRANGER'S HOUSE

Christin Lore Weber

WAKING

I WOKE ALONE, thinking nothing had happened, thinking the green curtains an ocean as they waved, forgetting where I was and why and with whom I might be living—a stranger I imagined I knew but never knew, pretending then, pretending now, constructing our reality on a breath, on a wave, and believing it.

I woke hearing his footsteps on the tile of the rooms beneath, hearing a door open and close, water poured, the stranger's voice, humming. Close to me I heard a clicking as of bones.

I woke lifting the sheets up and over my head, to hide, not from the stranger who had been kind, but from the spaces that had opened around me. No matter which direction I might turn I would find a precipice. Light through eyelids turns the morning red. Had there been a life before this room and the sounds beneath? Memory is a bird's wing. Memory is a stream. Memory is one lone tree.

I woke listening for the stranger's lighter steps now, coming up the stairs to where I lay awaiting him. When I lower the sheet from my eyes he will be standing there. This has happened before. I didn't know I needed him until he was present to me in a space I knew almost well but have forgotten, or that I

12

do forget and then forget again, a place that appears, then fades. I lower the sheet.

The stranger stands looking down at me. He is holding a wooden tray on which rest a bone china cup and a red rose in a simple crystal vase. "You are awake," he says, placing the tray on a bedside stand. "You are feeling better?"

I don't know how to answer.

When I look at him I see a man so familiar, so part of everything I am, so loved by me, that I am stunned to realize that I do not recognize his face. It is a face that could belong to anyone, although I do not mean that it is plain. Shall I say it is simple? That it is complex? It is both. It is simple as a deep, still pool, and complex as everything reflected there. I could search it, in it, all my life. This is what makes me think I love him.

"I brought tea and honey," he smiles

"And a rose." I smile back.

"Yes. From the rose garden by the kitchen path."

His eyes are deep and of a color that changes with what's around him. They are blue and green, light brown and gold. Since he brought me here, to this house, he's touched me only with those eyes.

I drink his tea and feel the heat of him pour into me. I desire him.

At first we touch while keeping air between us, our hands lifted in the solitude of air, feeling between us something almost firm, an energy, also pliant, living. Yes. As a rose petal lives, or a ball made of earth, or the moonlight if it could be held. Around that life we cup our hands, his and mine. "What is between us?" I ask.

"It is our one heart," he replies. "It is the heart of life."

Would it be possible to share everything this way? I didn't know. Could life be engendered in an exchange like this?

"Why am I here?" I ask.

"You had a husband," the stranger says, "And he died."

FLAKES OF MEMORY

I WASN'T SURE I loved the husband anyway. Up to the last minute, when I fastened the crown of wildflowers in my hair, straightened the skirt of my homemade dress with Granny's hand-crocheted inlays over my breasts and above my sacred parts, removed my shoes

14

to walk into the field (because the feet must not be confined upon the path), placed the dab of honey on my tongue to ward off sour words, clasped the necklace of shells around my neck to remind me of our origins, and performed all the other rituals everyone knew so well and had observed since the beginning— even as I did these things with all the purity my heart could muster, I wasn't sure. And ten years later, when he pushed his soul out through his head like a woman giving birth, I wasn't sure I cared.

Now I think I cared. Care. I care.

But the care is a demon I cannot exorcise.

MAKE LOVE TO ME

THE HUSBAND IS DEAD, but memory of the husband— more the fact of the husband, the husband's death— combines with the stranger's rituals of care and tears at me. Opens a vast chasm. I'd felt the emptiness before I knew what it might be. Now I feel the need to form something solid, beautiful. But the emptiness is not just within me or around me, it is me. Do I have skin? Bones? Life at all? I had spilled out of whatever had been my solidity. Before I can form anything, I need to be formed. I have no words for this.

The husband: he is dead.

I have not yet felt the horror of it, or I believe I did feel that horror, but if I did then why do I wake and pull the sheet up over my face and close my eyes to dispel whatever must not be seen? And yet I see the red. I am horrified at what lurks beneath my eyes.

The next morning after who knows how many mornings waking in the room with green curtains, when the stranger brings me tea and a rose, I say the only words I can that might come close.

"Make love to me."

The stranger sets the tray down on the stand. "Are you sure?"

"I'm sure."

This is how it began: The way he stood naked, the way he shone. I think it was the curls of lamplight that covered his skin. I'd never seen a penis uncircumcised, or how it rose as he walked towards me where I lay, or how I gasped when with himself he covered me.

Was it truly so? A hawk sheered the wind, lifting as I fell.

He did not leave that first day of this form of love, nor the next, but remained beside me in the bed,

16

reaching over to touch me, I never knew when he might. Nothing like this had happened to me ever before. It was as though I held my breath for hours. Under water. In the stratosphere. We would talk then and his words were hummingbirds flying in and out of my skin. His voice was the moaning of a storm through pines. I understood nothing.

Each time he leaves I get up from the bed and walk into a vacuum of gray space. It remains inside me. A suction. The absence. I dust the blue tile floor of his scroll room and stare into the endless air.

The curtains click like bones along the rod as wind lifts light green and the stranger makes his flowing way inside of me. Curtains lifting, falling and the click, click, click as the coffin closes and the key turns, locking. The stranger moving moving moving in out silken in my emptiness as the curtain lifts with a foreign wind while hands brush like billows on my skin.

I can feel the wind cooling the heat of loss.

The clicking of curtains becomes a language; what can be done? What cannot? It will take effort to silence the lock with its key that won't stop turning. I turn and drive my fingernails into the soft skin of the stranger who merges with me deeper, into a darkness where motion has no meaning. Silence even the heart's clicking. A red memory about to be released. Deeper yet, and the key breaks in the lock.

> *The widow has descended into the underworld.*
> *Beneath the surface of things.*
> *Her perspective on everything changes.*
> *She sees the world from the inside...*
> *She is a root woman...*
> *She is enclosed in the darkness of night,*
> *In the thick darkness of blood.*

CREEK

ON AN AFTERNOON I left the stranger's house and made my way to the creek. Normally I'd be afraid to venture out like that. I was afraid of everything after the husband's death. How I ever managed to reach the stranger's house remains a mystery to me, as though I do not know the woman who could do such a thing— accomplish it. The early winter rains had swollen the creek until it could be heard throughout the valley, tumbling over stones and fallen trees. I sat beside it where it turns south, then west again. The sun, interrupted here and there by the straight trunks of pines, played across my legs in bands of light and shadow. It warmed my face and breasts like touch. Like a fiery hand. The water roared. If I could be lost in it! If I could emerge from clothing like the moon moth from her cocoon and live even just one day. If I could be a fish and lower myself in the creek. A salmon coming home. Had I ever in my life been freely here? Even in the instant of that thought, fear turned me once again towards the stranger whose hands could smooth away the demon, and whose body could fill the demon's mouth. Even if my freedom had to be the price, I wanted him and the curls of his light touching my body. In the creek eddies of water curled like the stranger's hair, and I wanted him. I left my shoes at creek side and stepped into the water. I will be water, I told myself. I will be permeable to the sunlight. In and out of the swirling water I bent and turned and stood and bent again. The sunlight in the water entered me, rose up through all my openings like a different form of the stranger's body penetrating me everywhere. You can't imagine how it felt, the way death was washed away for at least that time while all I did was rise and fall, rise and fall, and water tumbled from me like curtains of silk billowing. I became nothing, naked, fluid light, translucent, shimmering.

Christin Lore Weber

THE STRANGER

THE STRANGER was unlike the husband and me in
every way. After just a few days I concluded that his
brain must be differently formed. The husband, on the
other hand, had held similar thoughts to mine. This
may have been part of the problem. This contrast may
also have been how the stranger tantalized. I'd been so
torn, crushed, stripped, turned to rags, muddied,
trampled, silenced, terrified, reduced, hollowed by
death that I welcomed the difference. I found I
welcomed lying back and being taken. The stranger
pinned my hands above my head with the strength of
one of his arms. He could have bound me with ropes or
satin ties; it would have calmed me. Strong did never
mean violent. No. Strong meant he would contain
while touching me feather light. So light. Another
form of light such as that shining in the waters of the
creek. He could make me long for that lightness while
being contained, immobilized, as he reached into me in
all the many ways he had, and all of them like water,
like feathers, like breath, like the tongue that forms
love's word or the lips that kiss so lightly that flames
leap climbing from bodily depths up, curling through
the body all the way through the heart, rushing
through lips and eyes, then bursting out in a

20

blossoming of stars. His strength was a tenderness to which I surrendered willingly.

He'd studied the arts of love during years spent in India and then Japan, with teachers skilled in the erotic arts. I learned little of those years in the ordinary way of chronicling. I learned the results of them, the breath, the music and the touch. Unlike the husband who had been taught the art of avoidance, the stranger possessed intimate knowledge of those connections between body and soul as well as the subtlety and skill of presence and awareness to intuit exactly the pace, the pressure of touch, the synchronizing of breath, to carry me beyond the mere physical to the higher pleasures of soul and spirit. I came to yearn for those extended days and nights in his presence and the waves upon waves of ecstasy on which he would take me away from the husband's recent death.

Everything I ever had been taught throughout my childhood and in my life before the husband married me in the field on that summer day in the presence of our community had forbid such erotic extravagance. It should have frightened me.

But death changes everything.

He touched me and I forgot.

Christin Lore Weber

WIDOW DREAM

FOR A WEEK the husband had been dead, and the stranger hadn't yet arrived. The dream shook me with the devil's claws, so stark it was, so nowhere I had ever been. In the end it was nowhere I'd known. It began at my home in my basement with the people of my life, living people and the dead, sitting in darkness, a circle on the earthen floor. A dark priestess in blood red vestments lit candles, giving one to each participant. Her veils were flame. Her feet were bone. She danced in the center and began chanting in a foreign tongue. The people joined her as the sound rose and fell, higher/deeper than the ear could tolerate. I'd been outside the circle, watching. My heart beat with the chant and the pounding of her feet. Then the circle opened and she came towards me, her hand outreached, and invited me into the center. I was given to understand this was my initiation, but into what I could not know. I followed her. The chanting rose in volume, deafening.

That power who exists in all beings as Shadow,
reverence to Her, reverence to Her, reverence to Her,
reverence, reverence.

She removed my clothes and wrapped me in her fiery veils. It was like a drug injected in my veins. The scene caught flame; it liquefied. The floor melted. We all

22

descended deeper. An abyss. It wasn't hell. I didn't know where we might be, but I knew it wasn't hell. Or, perhaps it was and I couldn't recognize it yet. Suddenly the chanting ceased. From the outer darkness I heard a mighty roar as of all air rushing into a vacuum, or as of a giant animal, wild and demanding. It appeared then from the edges, charging towards us in our smallness, a defenseless circle of the living and dead, and it a mighty god, the Sacred Bull, horns lowered.

Did I scream? Did I lie back knowing there could be no defense? I found myself outside the husband's bedroom door. Confused and terrified I stood alone. Suddenly his hand thrust out from the darkness to pull me in. I woke, struggling to get away.

SECRET

HER NAME may have been Wren who sat with me on the porch a few days only after the dream. We looked not at each other but rather out into the field. The alfalfa was in bloom. She was humming, "Blue skies up above..." Blue everywhere. Blue skies, blue field, and her eyes. Also the eyes of the husband, closed now. Maybe not even blue anymore. Wren's eyes, not exactly alfalfa blue, more periwinkle, into which I'd gazed over the years. Wren. We'd grown together in the community. Not always friends. I carried the perfect image of her in my mind. I could gaze on the alfalfa and still see her. Blue. I could imagine how the sunlight lit the barley tones in her long hair. I could almost hear her breath mixed with the hum of bees. This day tension beat between us. Heart. Vagina. The elemental pulse. The drumbeat of woman. We couldn't look on each other; it was forbidden. I thought of blue, fading. I thought of faded blue, the white of an eye, a globe into which the circle of blue has sunk.

"The death of a beloved is sexual abuse," Wren said. I couldn't help it then. I turned to her. Tears. Her face was wet with tears. Her blue eyes.

"What do you mean?"

"No one warns you," she turned to me, shaking her head. I wanted to touch her hair. "People say, 'He's with you in spirit,' but what you discover is that spirit has no cock." She paused. "I had a lover once..."

In the community such liaisons don't happen. Or if they do, no one speaks of them. Or the offenders disappear. He went to war right after high school and died.

"Hold me," she pleaded. We stood there on the porch in the blue of sky and of alfalfa. She moved towards me. She is taller than I and bent her head down, leaning against the side of my own. Her hair—

Later—after the feel of her heart beneath her dress, beneath her skin, beneath her firm breasts, beneath bone, beating—later we would let go and from then on we would not cease from gazing at each other deeply into eyes and through the eyes into something so concealed even a lover might not have seen. "…and you will long for him," she was saying. "Not just your emotions, certainly not simply your spirit, but your body will long for him. You will throb with emptiness like a woman whose child has died unborn. You will be hungry with the lack of him—his flesh, his fullness, his living body inside you. No one tells you this. God should be charged with sexual abuse for taking a lover in his youth. In our youth." We were silent for a long time. Gazing. Her breath. The bees.

"You can call me any time." She was leaving. "We can't give each other what we want—but, maybe, something…"

Yes. Wren. That must have been her name.

THE HUSBAND

AS I REMEMBER IT, he came upon me slowly in our youth. In the community even touch was thought forbidden. There were consequences. The body learns taboos. The body enthrones taboos in every cell and

25

reacts accordingly. This might not mean what you think. What it doesn't mean is this: that we could restrain ourselves. What it doesn't mean is also this: that we could freely embody and show our desire. So we proceeded slowly and in hiding. We knew a place in the woods where a cluster of birch trees grew. There we met. We lay in the grass or the dried leaves and tried what we could. Shy touches. Lingering kisses. I will not say I did not feel passion. I pulsed with it; it was forbidden. Restriction intensifies. He opened my blouse. He exposed my breast. Touch. Touch. His finger. His tongue. "I came," he confessed. "It was a flood of burgundy rushing through…" After that we chose to tell each other, no.

The very utterance of NO would bring it on. If it had not, if I'd had no passion for him at all, then I would wonder over the devastation of his death. Did death remove all barriers? Did every restriction that marriage failed to dissolve then melt? The hollowness of widowhood raved in me, a mouth that cried out without ceasing, could not be sedate.

I had thought I'd be sedate.

Widow's Walk

BETWEEN WORLDS

THE STRANGER ARRIVED quickly after Wren went away. Even now I believe this was necessary. If he had not come, what then? Even to today I believe I would have not survived. I believe the bony hand that reached from the husband's room would have drawn me in. It might have taken time, a year perhaps, before I would have slipped into the gray. But without doubt the Sacred Bull would need to break the bonds and bellow that world-altering cry.

I packed my suitcase just as a child might do when running from her home. I left it by the door and walked first to the wood because the birch trees there had been dear to me since childhood. As I recall, I spent some time sitting under them because how long I might be gone I couldn't know. At dusk I walked back home across the field.

The front door stood open. This seemed odd to me as I was sure I'd closed it. "Who's there?" I called, but no one answered. At the kitchen table sat the stranger. He had arrived and he removed me. You will ask me how; this I cannot tell you. It seems commonplace. A mere request. "Come with me to a different place. Come." I merely left my suitcase by the door. "You will need nothing," he said. "I will provide."

Christin Lore Weber

And he said to them, "Take nothing for your journey,
no walking stick, nor bag, nor bread, nor money;
and do not have two tunics.

I walked out my door and the piano disappeared. The table from my mother's house faded from my mind. Every book I'd ever owned, its pages documenting knowledge I'd assumed I would always hold within my mind. My clothes, my pottery dishes, my basket filled with yarn, the woven rug beside the door, the husband's wedding ring, the spray of wild grasses from his ritual of leaving. Gone. Gone. The community completely gone.

Except for Wren and few others, the community would have been no help to me. "Grief crazed her," the community would say. "Certainly she's been abducted. Do we even know the man? Didn't anyone suspect? Mark my words; she'll end up in a ditch somewhere." Wren, I know her, would have told me, Go.

The stranger opened his car door and motioned me to step inside. A little bell was ringing. An invitation. I heard a voice in my head, "Are you this daring?" And I was.

At the state line he stopped the car and turned to look at me. His eyes were the color of a meadow with flecks of goldenrod, and kind. "Are you sure?" he asked.

"I am," I answered.

"Good." He reached to me and placed his large hand over my smaller one for just the space of a breath. Then he started his car again and on we travelled into the west.

JOURNEY

YOU'LL WANT TO KNOW where we stopped to eat, which motels we favored, whether we saw the sights—the Grand Canyon, the Grand Tetons, what people we met along the way. It was not like that at all. I sang a bit. Opened the window to feel the breeze and smell the air as it changes when passing over different types of earth. It seemed my body changed its nature with each successive scent. It stored the grasses of the plains, and then the canyon rocks and spaces between them. The scent of rock, especially mammoth rock, is dense and filling. Of grasses, it's a hum. But the desert—there is mystery, and I took it in and savored it, the truth of it, the scent of truth. Water holds the various scent of every single thing. It transforms the earth's dying, a bit like fermentation, and I could smell the new arising. We drove off the road and spent an hour underneath a cottonwood tree beside a brown river.

Below the mountains at the ocean side he had his home. He led me through a room, bare but for large Japanese scrolls and some cushions, then up the stairs into his bedroom with the green silk curtains. He opened the windows behind them and the ocean breeze set them undulating, clicking in the faint way that would come to signal keen ecstasy haunted by a bonelike voice of death.

And here I am.

WIDOW DREAM

THE HUSBAND COMES to me by night while the curtain bones click away, nights while the stranger sleeps, nights of crashing surf and then the surf quieting as it ebbs. I hear the wind through the seaside grasses and the deep voice of the foghorn a mile down the beach at the jetty. Nothing can stop him then, though I think he doesn't know where he's come as he comes. I think he thinks the stranger's bed his own and that he lies beside me back home, with the prairie grasses filtering the wind's moan.

It doesn't seem a dream, my lying between them, the husband gray and gruesome, not knowing he has died. The stranger long and golden. The husband's face contorted as it was that moment of his soul emerging on his last ragged breath. The ugliness feels unbearable. He presses himself against me, wanting *in*. No-oh-no. I cannot bear him there. His stink of death. His bloated belly. The awful gray of him. And worst of all that he does not know. He wants intercourse, to travel the rivers of life in me, and he will, in that journey, pollute me with his death.

Leave me! Leave! But his arms wrap me like ropes. You are dead, I want to tell him but my mouth is filled with leaves.

THE DEER SCROLL

MORNINGS, after such dreams, I retire to the stranger's large scroll room that overlooks the sea to sit quietly on a silk cushion and gaze upon the deer scroll. After such horror, delicacy. How can I make sense of it?

Once in the time before, at the edge of the alfalfa field, a herd of white tailed deer roamed paths just inside a bordering stand of birch. The husband stood beside me on the porch as sunset tinged the sky the many colors of burnt orange to simmering lemon.

We watched them step into the open, a slender line of beauty and of grace. We were past the autumn equinox and the fawns we'd watched scampering in spring now had lost their camouflage and followed in a more stately way their mother doe. "Look," he whispered with excitement. "Look." I remember now how he had an eye for loveliness. Darkness unfolded over the field.

That night we were awakened by a pounding. The husband rose from bed and I followed him towards the noise. It led us to the porch. He took the flashlight and went outside to inspect. He looked shaken. "It's one of the fawns," he said. "I think it's dying."

"But we just saw them all this evening." I could not take it in. "They were well; I know that they were well. How could one be dying?"

He couldn't explain it either and crouched down. To be nearer to the creature he laid his hand on the young deer's flank. "Peace," he said. "What's happening is never long to be endured." And I thought then that the young one knew human intention and took comfort from the husband's voice. "I'll stay," he said, whether to me or to the deer I'll never know. Then, "I'll keep watch. You get some sleep. I'll let you know."

He must have wanted to be alone with this— this mystery. I returned to bed as he wished me to do, and just before sunrise I sensed he was again with me in our room. "He's gone," he told me in a low voice. He sat, then, on the edge of our bed, put his head into his hands, and wept.

He had an eye for loveliness. At Summer Solstice of the following year he himself was gone, just as suddenly.

In the stranger's house I gaze upon the deer scroll. Deep, deep in my being I feel the absence of all knowing. The deer. The husband. Something about loveliness. Then the horror of my dream.

At night I ask the stranger about his deer scroll. What does it mean? We stand before the scroll. "The deer comes as a divine messenger," he says. "It's a Shinto belief. When the deer comes to you it is as a prophet of the sacred mystery of God."

DEAREST WREN

YOU MAY BE WONDERING where I am.
Possibly you are worried. Don't worry.
 I'm writing because I have some questions about the husband, When he was alive,

Christin Lore Weber

During those years, the years before.

Amazing to hear from you.
People have asked.
Of course I'm worried.
All of us are worried.
Where are you?
Your postmark is unrecognizable.

Somewhere by the ocean—I'm not sure.
I leave my postcards by the door and they are mailed.
You knew him all the years, and you knew me—
I can't find him in me anymore.
The one I see in dreams
Is dark.
Was he a form of darkness—before?

There were times
He kept his silences
He wandered in the birch stand
A shadow;
Other times he danced.

When will you return?

I may not
Return.

PATH

GRASSES TOWER above me on the path. It is a labyrinth winding to the sea. At times it crosses itself. Sea flowers, single and on bushes, color the way. Yellow Scotch Broom, Indian Paint Brush, Wild Iris, orange and red Poppy, clusters here and there of Sea Lilies. On the rocks above the path the cypress, sculpted by the ocean winds, giant bonsai master. I walk the path in every weather. I walk it starting on the rocks underneath those trees when morning fog clings to branches in the stillness and the great blue heron can be seen through the mists where she balances on a ruined limb of a drifting cedar log. I walk it in wind and pelting rain making wet ropes of my hair. It stings my skin, tiny stones of wet, terrible scream of storm through the cypress above, relieving me, match for match the feeling of it. Widow-maker storm and the widow herself, whipped, wounding, wounded. Yes. Oh, I welcome it. I also walk the path in sunlight—beetles on the blades of grass.

Today I take the path under the cypress trees down the rocky natural stairs to the sand dunes where the grasses wave in a light ocean breeze. The day is quiet. The stranger rose early while I still slept, and he is gone. Many mornings I awaken to solitude like this. Whether it is simply the way of things or a plan the stranger has devised for me, I never know nor ask. The rocky descent switches back and forth for safer footing, so I don't see the deer until she and I stand face to face. She doesn't startle but stands in unearthly stillness, her eyes like the eyes of a natural divinity. Messenger. Whatever has been in me of myself vanishes in her gaze. Her stillness — how can I say it? — isn't stationary. Her leap and all the sudden energy of it seem encapsulated. It is alive, already happening but contained, as though time has stopped mid-motion. And I, too. What has been of me has either not arrived yet on the scene, or it has gone on into a future past our meeting there. Messenger. Maybe what we see is recognition. Something lost or gained. Something present but not known—not possible to know. We stand. That is all.

REVEALED

I TELL THE STRANGER. In the absolute dark without even the moon's light over the water beyond the curtains, I tell him, "He's come for me, wants to take me. I'm afraid." He says nothing. I feel his breath, wet on my skin. Breath moves across my body, softening. Time ceases to have meaning. Where my body softens, soon it dissolves. The stranger, too, disappears and only the breath remains. In the darkness only breath moves, only breath remains moving over me, touching each part 'til it dissolves, flows, is rain evaporating, being taken up. We are together, breath. No world but breath.

"Where did you learn this?" I ask him afterwards as we recline on a down comforter against the silk pillows in the scroll room, drinking chardonnay from glasses blown into slender tubes. He wears a robe of Asian design and has one knee cocked so that the robe lies open around it, revealing that entire leg while concealing the other. I think how strong he is—alive. We had lit candles, and their flames reflect in the windows, the wine glasses, and on his skin. The ocean pounds the sand and rock. He'd wrapped me in a coverlet of woven raw silk when we left the bed.

"I told you, I spent time in India, in Japan."

"Yes, but really—who can do these things?"

He is silent.

"What kind of person can bring the body and soul together? Who can bring another person to such a place as—

"Um…"

"As you just did with me? You made death disappear."

"No..." he murmurs. "No, that's not what happens." He puts his wine glass on the floor beside the comforter, then takes my glass also from my hand and puts it aside. "You will need to let go of categories. Your thought has been built on them as if on bricks. Life or death—they don't exist like that. I don't take death away; I go into death with you to pass through a boundary of space and time into deeper being. All that is needed is an opening like breath or tears or touch or perhaps the click of the curtains or that hawk's cry you've been hearing."

He reaches over and slowly drags the edge of the silk coverlet down across my right breast. The rawness of unrefined silk caresses the tiny hairs on my skin, already beginning to arouse me. "The body is a path," he says so low and deep his voice is far away thunder over mountains. "Sex reaches its fulfillment when you realize it is more than sensation, more than love, more than procreation, more than worship even. Sex is an opening through the ravishment of death into the Nothing, the NoSpace, the NoTime, of Ultimate Reality. Sex can set us on this path when the partners have at least a daring willingness of heart to endure the descent of surrender, together, not to each other but to the darkness and within that darkness to a divine transformation from which they emerge as the bodily being of God." He gazes into my eyes. "You are experiencing the first step upon this path today. The dissolution into breath."

The image of the husband appears in my mind. I'd wanted him gone. But if the stranger's words are true, then it is that image and my revealing it that opened the way for what had happened to me only an hour or so before. The husband is a part of this, this...I don't know what. Despite the stranger's attempt to explain it to me, I have little experience to support his words.

"Shall we continue?" He smiles.

"I want to," I respond. My body certainly is willing; by now I can feel the surf pounding right inside of me.

"Breathe," he says, uncovering my breast completely. I watch him lower his head. I feel his tongue barely touch and then circle slowly around the aureole. The candles flicker. His hand slides under the silk cover, down past my belly, and rests on the Mound of Venus, quiet at first, no movement, then just the slightest pressure alternates with relaxation. One finger only. Finger and tongue, and the pounding of the surf. So this is touch. The beginning of touch. How long does it last? However long, his touch opens the path once again, and I am flowing on it towards the darkness. When time is no more and space is lost in

Christin Lore Weber

nothingness, his finger passes through into the watery places and I surrender.

THE ROCK

AT THE END of the path where at high tide long leaves of kelp wash onto the sand and stay to dry in the heat of day, a rock stands. Perhaps it had crashed from the cliff above it during some seismic shift long enough ago to have become encrusted with barnacles and sea moss, long enough even to have been intimate with wind and tide before any human creature climbed its jagged body to sit in the smooth indentation that serves as a chair above the waves. I find myself there on a late-summer afternoon. Except for the gulls and the always present hawk that makes her nest in the largest cypress on the cliff, I am alone.

The ocean sings the endless song of the planet earth. Other songs there are, contrapuntal, but not continuous. The ocean sings a love song to the land, the same song without end. I listen. Had I done nothing else forever?

I have the husband on my mind. Had I known that he would die and done nothing? If I'd known, or even suspected that I knew, and still done nothing, even to not questioning him with a word—"You're

40

looking tired, dear. When was the last time you saw your doctor?"—so simple it would have been. If I said nothing, and yet I knew somewhere in the inchoate depths of myself, had I then not played some part in his death? And if I did, why? These are thoughts that friends like Wren warn against. But does anyone have that kind of power? Can people really die from not being loved enough?

Did I love him?

I married him that day in the field. Would I marry him again? What question must I ask that will produce the answer that I seek to understand?

A child never born comes to me in dreams. Every time she comes I know her as though I'd held her growing inside my body, not like in a dream that twists and fades and morphs from one to another being within the same phantasmagoric world. No. She is real. Within the dream she remains constant as who she is.

I know, as though in the dream I have historical memory, knowing in my very cells all the many moments of my child's life, from birth to when I wake. And when I wake I am stricken with such grief. I wake in tears, sometimes sobbing, disconsolate. I am Mary when the rock is rolled to the door of the tomb. My heart is torn from my body. I cannot walk. I can barely breathe. I am Rachel mourning for her children and they are no more. The loss of my child is my greatest grief. Far greater than the husband's death.

Did we make the child together? I remember as I sit above the ocean on the rock, tide coming in, how we lay in the blue alfalfa of the Before. The blazing sun.

His hands on me were cool.

I cannot see his face.

THE BEFORE

I SAW THE HEAT lift off the field in waves of light startling the grass. Blue dragonflies stitched it all into a piece. Inside the house I made quilts in patterns passed down, family designs, fabric cut from wedding dresses worn before my birth and tablecloths used only on holidays. Sometimes a baptismal gown. A stained party dress. A man's silk tie. A few things can be saved this way. Remember.

Mostly and already the waves of light rise and seem to disappear. The husband in the field. The blue become gold become chaff lifting up as dust. The field mouse running towards a bale. Wren singing as she walks up the gravel road home from town. Will she also fade? I can't stop the fading; a reality I didn't want to know.

Widow's Walk

Flakes of memory bring life back again. Even while the husband disappears.

DEAR WREN

Remember how you would sing
Coming up the road?

That did happen
Then. One day I stopped
Singing.

I still can see you through the heat
Through the summer light
How your body turned to water
layers of color singing
Above the dirt road.

I wanted nothing more
Than for you
To hear.

I did hear.
I wanted nothing more
Than to reach my hand
To touch your hair

43

Christin Lore Weber

To undo your hair

I'd bound my hair.

You'd bound your hair
And I had bound my tongue
I'd bound my heart
I'd stitched together all desire
To touch
You.

It was forbidden

Much had been forbidden
Remember how the slightest breeze…

Reminded us…

Of love.

THE COMMUNITY

THE PEOPLE had a way. This way was not a path, but I didn't know that before. It was a blackberry thicket. Remember the sweetness that stained. Remember the thorns that drew a thin line of blood up and down the arm.

44

THE FIELD

IF I COULD lie down in the field, perhaps I could be well. If I could lie down. If in the field the wind could be a husband to me; if the dragonfly could be my god. If the hand of rain could wash me, if rain could settle the dust, settle the haunting voice of dust, settle the clicking of the bones—bury them like seed. Could I then go round and back, or is retracing never something to be done?

Who is the husband standing in the wavering heat of the field?

Into the field we walked together. I wore a crown of wildflowers in my hair. My dress was a quilt of fabrics that went back to the beginning through the fingers of all whose faces had formed my own. No one gave me away. I gave myself. A child held my hand. And I walked barefoot into the field on a day that sunlight wavered all the way to the first birch tree appearing through the light as though it danced. Wren sang her song. And the child walked between us, the husband and me, into the field.

THE ROCK

AM I WHO I AM? Around me swirls salt water at high tide. On the rock I've lost track of time and of myself. The sun is setting and the light weave of this dress I'm wearing will not protect me from a wind turned cold. It is time to take the path back to the stranger's house. I wonder as I climb to the swirling water at the bottom of the rock if I am here at all. My bare feet touch the swirl. Surf, not so far away now, pounds and moves the sands. I feel the answering woman-drum. How can it not be real?

As I follow the path up through the grasses to the rock stair, I feel the emptiness again and wonder if the stranger will be there to greet me when I reach the house. Already I am hungry for his touch.

As I reach the topmost rock of the natural stair I hear the fluid keening of the hawk. I look up, but I see nothing flying there.

ABSENCE

TILES ON THE KITCHEN FLOOR are slate blue, irregular as though pried loose from the mountain on a summer afternoon and laid down here underneath my feet. I go through each room of the house looking for the stranger. As he wasn't there when I woke in the morning, so he isn't there as the day comes to a close. If he is returning from the city he will welcome dinner at the round oak table in the alcove above the water.

I gather food of every color: a fresh red salmon filet with its silver skin, a lemon yellow as rays of sun, green spring lettuce, white feta cheese, deep purple aubergine, sprigs of lavender and rosemary, raspberries black and red, thick coddled cream, golden sherry amontillado wine. Each food tastes of its color, of the combination of scents, and I anticipate its transformation by the oven's flame. Each recipe in its dish resembles an artwork when I set it on a shelf in the ice closet. Each will be freshly baked, and not too much, once the stranger has returned.

I sit in the scroll room to wait.

The sunset casts a path of copper over the ocean all the way to where it disappears at the horizon, and then night falls. The water below the cliff changes hue to lapis, then purple then impenetrable black. Even more deeply than the dark I feel the loss of him, but pretend normalcy. I rise from the cushion by the windows and return to the kitchen to open the bottle of sherry, pour myself a glass, and return to the scroll room to light a candle. The fog horn on the jetty acts as a depth finder in every one of my cells.

Where is he? I sip the sherry and I think of death.

Only when I wake do I realize that I've slept. Maybe he's returned and, not wanting to disturb me, gone to bed. In the bedroom only the sea green curtains undulating. "Are you here?" I call, but am answered by the clicking of the bones.

A flare of anger. How could he do this? He should realize how already death has reamed me. What could be his purpose if he realizes that? Surely he knows what his sudden absence would mean, how the nothingness would call the husband from his grave. Cruel. Cruel to love me as he's done and then to disappear. To bring me to this place, out of my home, away from the blue fields, to this hard place, this place of rock and sand and crashing surf, this place of the hawk that circles. Why? To bring me to this place, away from Wren, away from everything I'd ever known. Who is he?

My stomach turns. It holds nothing but vertigo. I fall as I run towards the bathroom. I get to my knees, and to my feet, and make it through the doorway. Leaning over the sink my body tries to turn itself inside out. But all that comes out of me is empty air.

PIA

A VOICE. "Are you home?" A woman's voice. A clarinet voice, reedy. Sinuous. Another call, "I've brought some wine and cheese. I thought we could sing a bit, dance, feed one another like birds."

"Oh!" I come out of the bathroom and stand in the center of the scroll room as she enters through the door connecting it to the kitchen. "Who are you?"

"I might ask you the same," she lifts her right eyebrow over mischievous green eyes, iridescent as underwater moss. Then she laughs. "Just a neighbor," she charms. "And you?"

"A house guest, you might say."

"Oh…okay." She bends her head to the side, surveying me, then floats towards me like a cottonweed seed on wind. She holds out her hand. Multi-colored bracelets dangle from her arm. Her clothes flow, feminine, soft layers of red, purple, blue and green. An exotic bird. Feathers. The firebird, I think, suddenly excited. She takes my hand, lifts it to her mouth and kisses my fingers one by one.

"A-n-g-e-l…" she draws it out. "Is he here?"

"I don't know where he is. Actually, I haven't seen him since night before last," I say, trying to cover with smooth tones a quaver of uncertainty.

"Don't be alarmed," the neighbor sits down on one of the cushions. "He's a bit of a wanderer, you know, a pilgrim, a lover of adventure. It gives him his charm and whatever else it is he has—call it mystery?" Both of us are quiet for a moment, then, as if thinking of it for the first time she blurts out, "Oh! And my name is Pia. What's yours?"

When had I last spoken my name aloud? Did I even know my name anymore, since the husband died? Did I even want my name, that same name, the one belonging to the Before? "I don't remember, but I think it started with a B," I tell her as I realize it is true.

"Then I'll call you Beatricé," she says as though having never realized one's own name is considered commonplace. "Dante's beloved angel is what I saw when you appeared and I took your hand. Who knows? Maybe that's what you are, the angel of beauty in a fleshly form—I see the world sometimes as though I'm looking through a telescopic lens in which everything is present at once, connected in a way that as the aperture increases I begin to see that everything is hidden inside everything else. Maybe there's an angel hidden somewhere deep in you and she feathered forth as Beatricé in the moment I pronounced your name."

Widow's Walk

Pia reaches out and takes my hand. "You aren't busy, are you? Let's walk to the creek and get to know each other."

We take the same path I'd taken earlier up the mountain. A deer path, I believe, narrow but well trodden between embedded rocks pock-marked with lichen. Sunlight angles through the mountain laurel and the pines. Are we two exotic birds skimming the rocks, lifting now and then, weightless with memory and thought, but unaware. Aware only of our voices, the pattern of them like polyphony winding around and through, Hildegard and Richardis, wings touching, feathers on the breath of God. Either we are new or never old. From wherever we came to end up here, in this place, on this ascending rock, neither of us know. If we have known each other somewhere, maybe in another life, maybe in our minds and hearts according to the drift of many people's most esoteric philosophies, neither of us know for sure. Here's what we know: to touch each other is the same as lightly running fingers over our own skin. To speak, as though we put form to the drift of one another's spirit. We enter each other's life that day as though both of us are newly born upon this earth, and as though we are of all women the most ancient, split off in the beginning from the eternal One. Red rose and white. Firebird and dove.

"I had a friend in the Before. Her name was Wren," I say to her.

"I've had no friend here, in this place, until this moment," Pia responds.

How could we know? An hour passes, at most two hours.

We arrive at the creek by the place where it leaves the steep where the water turns wild, and from there it tumbles more calmly towards the thick woods. We sit on the rocks, light breezes lifting our hair, sunlight warming us. We set our shoes aside on the bank and let the water cool our bare feet and let the hems of our skirts drift in the current.

"Tell me about the Before," she says.

THE BEFORE

"IN THE BEFORE WAS THE HUSBAND, the community, and a friend named Wren. The fields were there and a road that led to a small town. Wren walked the road each day, singing, and her voice made circles with the wind. I breathed the air made sweeter by her voice.

"The husband tilled the alfalfa field that turned from black to green to blue to gold to white according to the seasons. We married in the field and made love on the alfalfa flowers flattened into a blue blanket by our bodies' weight. There ought to have been children. I can see a child in visions now, but I can't remember her. She walks with him, but I don't know where she is and her name is lost to me. This troubles me.

"The husband is a blur, but he appears in dreams. He is dead but still he speaks. When he lived in the Before I believe that he was kind. He was silent and he was kind.

"I was lonely—desperately.

"I don't know what I needed that I didn't have.

"Then the husband died, and of that my memory is confused—obscured. Time dissolved. The stranger came and brought me here. It's all I know."

"It's enough for now," Pia says. "It is, perhaps, too much for one heart to bear."

She slips off the rock into the water, and I follow her. It isn't deep. We lie floating just above the bottom like salmon. Our hair fans out in the current. Our clothes drift like the tails of tropical fish.

She holds my hand.

Christin Lore Weber

FLUTE

WHEN I WALK through the doorway to the stranger's house, I hear the haunting music of a wooden flute. Below the deep breathing music the constant beat of surf. I stand, opened by these living sounds to the core of being. Closing my eyes I am still. He is entering me this way as the tone flutters, returning to me something fluid of myself. I stand on the slate blue tile of the stranger's house losing and finding myself in the long, sensuous tones.

COMMON PLACE

Christin Lore Weber

EXODUS

BIRDIE MACKENZIE ARRIVED FIRST at the little
Common Place Church for the regular Saturday Bible
study. Pastor Joseph didn't keep the doors locked
because there had never been a need out in the
grasslands of North Dakota to distrust one's
neighbors. At least not until the recent disappearance.
But so far no one had mentioned that unwelcome
mystery. No one in the Common Place township
wanted to be thinking such a thing, so foreign to
everything anyone had been brought up to believe.
They were farmers and ranchers out here where the
Great Plains began. Most of the families had settled
around Common Place as homesteaders coming west in
Calistoga wagons, and the cemetery beside the little
church was populated with those forbearers and often
the tiny graves of their infants and small children who,
for reasons of illness or weakness or weather, didn't
make it into their safer years.

    Their church was what might be called a
conglomerate congregation. Little bits of belief from a
variety of more established denominations—usually
but not always Christian—took root in what the
founders called a common place. Thus the church's as
well as the township's name. Mostly this dovetailing of
various doctrines made an acceptable weave, and

people were tolerant. Pastor Joseph had been with them for almost twenty years and except for lately had managed their boundaries of belief with gentleness and wisdom. He had been a good shepherd, accessible and kind.

Birdie had been born in Common Place, as had the other women in regular attendance at the Saturday Bible Study, all but Miss Mathilde who lived in the town of Greenleaf, seven miles down the road at the turn-off to the highway going towards Fargo. Miss Mathilde brought a Presbyterian perspective to the group, as well as an educated mind, having graduated with honors from the University in Grand Forks. Her status as grade school teacher gave her a position of some authority within the group.

Birdie opened the church door and smelled the familiar odor of oiled and polished wood mixed with the everlasting scent of fields, rich soil and natural fertilizer. She turned to the right and took the stairs into the basement. The Bible Study group always met down there. It was a community hall, of sorts, where the Common Place folks held pot luck dinners, bazaars, the monthly meetings of the men's association and the women's guild. The old stone walls kept the basement cool in summer and would be a welcome respite from heat and humidity for all four women who would probably attend on this day.

Usually there would have been five, but Birdie's dear friend, Bee Fenelon, wouldn't be coming. She had vanished. Birdie still hadn't adjusted to Bee's absence and probably never would.

This was the first Bible Study since Bee disappeared, and Birdie couldn't imagine how she might get through the two hours of discussion. She opened the door to the utility closet and took out four chairs which she placed in a circle, then she sat to wait. Sunlight streamed through the dust on the narrow basement window. Birdie made a mental note to clean those windows before Sunday Services the next day. The women who volunteered to clean the church on Fridays must have missed that little task. She'd do it. She didn't mind. She knew that if she forgot sometime when she was volunteering another woman would pick up the slack for her.

She stared at the other three chairs. There ought to have been four still empty. Five in all. What had happened to Bee?

When Bee Fenelon disappeared only a little over a month after her husband died no one even noticed at first. She was a bit of a stay-at-home anyway. She preferred her books to most people. It seemed hard for her to welcome company even in the hard times. The first few days after the death, the women of Common Place brought the usual hot dishes and cake, and she received the kindnesses at the door, but invited no one in. Some of the men also visited, prompted by the Bible admonition to care for the widow. They tried not to bother her even with a knock. They knew she could see them from the kitchen window as they made sure the fields were okay and checked the farm equipment.

Birdie had visited and was invited in. She and Bee went way back. School friends. Graduated together almost twenty years before. Birdie and her husband Bud stayed close to Bee and Will all the years that followed. Folks living both in Greenleaf and the township of Common Place are known for their loyalty. Despite Bee's little personality quirks, everyone took it hard when they heard she'd gone missing. People tend to blame themselves. Most of them don't say it out loud but in their heads that nagging voice keeps saying things like "I could have done this," or "why didn't I do that?"

Some thought she might be lying dead somewhere, maybe even have taken her own life. You can't tell what a woman might do when her husband dies. Grief eats at the mind of anyone, gets anyone confused. For weeks folks talked in low voices about how little they knew her, really, the way that she'd gotten more and more private the older she became.

There might be things so private that even Birdie didn't know. What if she had gone out somewhere in the birch woods and taken a handful of those pills Doc Johnson gave her to help with grief's nausea? The rumor started that Birdie Mackenzie had agreed that pills might have been the answer everyone was looking for. And Birdie knew Bee. So for a while the folks searched the woods near her house, but didn't find a thing. Bud found a dead deer half eaten by something, but that was it. No one found even a trace of Bee.

Some said there ought to be a second memorial service, but most thought that such a notion showed disrespect and that it was traditional to wait seven years at least before declaring any missing person dead. Birdie had told Granny Jarvis how she'd been sitting with Bee on the porch, and Bee just kept staring out over the alfalfa field, choking every time she tried to talk about Will. She ought to have thought before saying anything, especially to Granny, for whom bits of information were a currency she liberally passed around. Gently, of course. Lovingly. Wanting everyone to share the joys and sorrows of them all. Most folks understood. Such a sudden loss. Horrible, really. Who could blame the woman even if she were to run away, leave Common Place? Everything she looked at must have reminded her.

Widow's Walk

She could have been abducted—the most intolerable of possibilities because of people's ingrained sense of safety, so most in the community wouldn't hear of it. She was a plain woman, and with no money to speak of despite the land and the alfalfa crop. Cash poor, they argued—unlikely to be taken like that because what would be the benefit? Some did think it odd, though, that her door stood open and her car sits right there in the drive to this day.

Miss Mathilde came down the stairs right at two o'clock, and Marnie Cole was with her. They always arrived together, carpooling from Greenleaf where both of them now lived. Karyn Nyström arrived a few minutes later. Everyone looked more than a little shaken by the fact that Birdie only put out four chairs, as well as a bit chagrinned by the implications of both her action and their response.

To begin with, nothing was said of their missing friend. Miss Mathilde launched into their subject for the day, the book of *Exodus*. The very name of the book, all of a sudden, caused an electrical current to run through each of them. Had Bee Fenelon deliberately made her exodus from Common Place? No one mentioned it. Karyn cast a meaningful glance at Birdie. Miss Mathilde asked, like the teacher she was, "What do you think this verse in the exodus of the

Jews from Egypt means for us?" And she opened her Bible and read, "And the Lord went before them by day in a pillar of cloud to lead the way, and by night in a pillar of fire to give them light, so as to go by day and night. He did not take away the pillar of cloud by day or the pillar of fire by night from before the people."

Birdie immediately thought of Bee walking through a wilderness in the dark of night, and she burst into tears.

"Oh, Birdie!" Marnie produced a clean hankie from her pocket and handed it to her. "We all feel just awful. I'm sure all of us could spend this entire hour crying." Already tears were flowing down Karyn's face, but quietly, as though she weren't aware of them. And Miss Mathilde was murmuring that really they ought to have changed the topic for the day and she was so sorry for having even asked them to consider that quotation, though any quotation from the topic of the exodus was bound to have reminded them of Bee.

It was clear that they would not be discussing the exodus of the Jews on that Saturday, but would be trying to deal with the awful emptiness in their group, in their hearts. And the grief and fears started pouring out of them, the feelings that had floated to the surface, first, and then the initial evidence of even deeper concerns.

Who could sort out now who said what things? So much speculation had been rising here and there in the entire region. It was difficult anymore to remember if they heard something from another person or had conjured it inside their own minds. Sometimes they'd insert little bits of gossip they'd heard about Will and Bee, little disagreements and such, maybe some talk they weren't sure Bee had heard, or heard too late. They excused themselves from being gossips with the pure fact that they needed to collect every bit of information they could if they ever expected to find Bee again and bring her home. It honestly struck the entire group of them as the Christian thing to do, even though secretly some of them weren't exactly Christian at all. But what choice did they have? No one would have thought to answer any other way if she were to be asked, and this despite the unusual conglomeration of beliefs woven into the foundation of their little church. And for a Christian, to find out what had happened to Bee Fenelon was the absolutely necessary thing to do. A loving thing. The believing thing. Faithful. Hopeful. "Faith is the substance of things hoped for," quoted Birdie, "and the evidence of things unseen." No one could doubt that Bee had become a thing, or rather a person, unseen. Would they follow the Bible or not? Actual churchgoers or not, they must. No question.

Birdie actually had started the interrogations of her own memories, as soon as her weeping subsided, with stories of her own, as was only right, as she was Bee's best friend. Also she'd been almost equally hurt by Will's death because she and Bud spent more time with the Fenelon's than anybody else. It broke her heart those days last winter, after the initial surgery, sitting with Bee at the hospital in Fargo just waiting, breath by breath, in case poor Will might die that very day. Bee and herself. Bud stayed home. He had some excuse, but Birdie expressed her opinion that men take it hard in a different way than women do, as though death is a personal affront and they ought to have prevented it. They always seem to be at war with something, and that's why they come back from the real war in Viet Nam so messed up because of what they saw and how they couldn't stop it from happening. And afterwards they seem to need to stop it everywhere, and sullenness or anger overtake them when they discover over and over again that they can't.

As it turned out, death right during or after that surgery might have been the better thing. Maybe

Bee would still be here but for that one (granted it was horrific) detail.

Birdie would have kept on going but for Marnie Cole who broke in right over what Birdie was saying. "I can't help it, but I miss her so much." Marnie was a large young woman with the prettiest skin. She'd been a pretty baby, too—round as a peach and soft, the older women in the church were fond of saying. It was too bad, they thought and often said aloud, the way nature tends to exaggerate as we age. But anyway, pretty is as pretty does.

"Maybe guilt took her away from us. I mean, what if she felt relief that he was finally gone and she was free. It can happen." Marnie blushed, knowing she had gone a bit too far.

The other women's heads had snapped towards her at the very mention of that word, guilt. Not that they hadn't thought it, but... Guilt, relief, those were an accusation. If Bee had been at Bible study, no one would dare to so much as suggest such things. But now it was said, well, thoughts rose up in every woman's mind. Maybe her own thoughts from just the way a husband is—maybe having memories of Bee, who as a child actually wasn't all that reclusive, but afterwards began to lock herself away behind a stoic face that revealed less and less each year. By the time Will died who knew whom she'd become? Even Birdie—did she know? She acted like she knew, took pride in knowing, but she'd always been a dramatic sort. Since girlhood she'd been the best story-teller in the town, making up and presenting talent shows and plays; she was good at that, and everyone enjoyed it without even thinking that the art of making stories out of life, according to some, was just another word for long, drawn out lies.

The women didn't like to think of Bee running off somewhere as though the folks in Greenleaf and Common Place weren't good enough to help her through this trial. The very thought of it set them to defending her in their minds. And some of those thoughts tumbled out into the study group.

"I've heard that people, when grief hits really hard, can suffer from amnesia," Karyn Nyström, another classmate of Bee and Birdie, but never married and always a bit lonely herself, commented as she blushed just from hearing her own voice. "Wouldn't that be awful? Just imagine ..." She could say no more, fearful of herself possibly falling into a situation such as that. Why, Karyn remained reluctant to drive to town for fear she might get lost, even though she'd been a passenger on every single road in the county since the moment of her birth—literally. Her momma brought her forth in her daddy's pickup, during a rainstorm, stuck in the mud on one of those very roads. She had never recovered from the trauma of it. She didn't trust her father from that day on, nor from the looks of it, any other man.

Somehow Karyn's comment made the best sense of all to everyone, and also took them back, with no small relief, to the book of Exodus, and the way God seems to set folks down in the wilderness without a bite to eat or water to drink except what falls from the sky or comes out of the stone. It all seemed a bit much for any of them to take completely seriously, but at the same time gave each of them a small token of their own relief as of a place to rest from what had maybe been their own responsibility. God did send those pillars of light and shadow though.

Dear Bee. Lost.

Birdie realized later, as she was driving Bud's old red pickup down the road towards her home, singing out the open window as she often did, songs like "The Old Rugged Cross," and "In the Garden," that she'd begun to think of Bee as someone she'd never see again. It was a magical sort of thinking and something she believed a person shouldn't do. Secretly she suspected that such thoughts could make the thing you thought of come to be. It wasn't as though paganism hadn't been woven into the foundations of the church along with everything else, but the people at the present day Common Place Church barely recognized it for what it was, the weaving was so well-wrought and close. They would think she might be possessed or practicing occultism if they knew she thought that way. But magic actually happened around her now and again. The time the tree fell on Mike Munson and bashed his head in to name just one. She'd just been thinking about the possibility of that very thing only a day before it happened. It wasn't exactly Mike Munson in her thought, but just any of the men working on the new electric lines and clearing trees standing in the way, that they should be more careful and not tempt fate by walking where they shouldn't or leaving their yellow hard hats in the truck. He died. She still took a bit of responsibility for that. It was one of those sins you can't tell a soul but God for fear your little bit of craziness will be found out. Who would trust you ever again? Oh her, the folks would say, the crazy one, believes her thoughts will cause the trees to fall. Why, despite the tolerance and inclusiveness of Common Place, there were limits. If they started suspecting her of witchery, she'd have to move to a different town.

Those thoughts stopped her short. She stopped singing right at "while the dew is still on the roses" and said out loud, "Bee, I'll bet you went off to another town because you thought Will died because of something you *thought*."

Widow's Walk

Bee sometimes hadn't much liked him. Birdie knew this about her friend. It was clear to Birdie that thoughts could be deadly as a virus or a falling tree. As thoughts pile up they get stronger and maybe can cause the flu or pneumonia or cancer. She had heard Bee express such powerful thoughts sometimes when they sat together on the porch. "I don't mind that Will doesn't talk to me much. Truth be told, I prefer him silent." She'd said that once—maybe even more. Or, "I wish I'd have taken up writing poetry instead of being someone's wife, but then you can't eat poetry, can you? Or sleep between its lines." Isn't it dangerous to say such things? It got worse. "I wish he wouldn't touch me anymore." Even Birdie knew you never should say such a thing as that. That kind of wish could be the evil magic that sets the virus multiplying beyond control.

Birdie drove the rest of the way without singing. She passed by Bee's house off across the harvested field but didn't turn her head to look at the empty porch. She was pretty sure right then that Bee had murdered Will with her thoughts and afterwards took the first opportunity to get distance between herself and what she had done. And so she left her entire old life behind, car still sitting there in the drive so she would not be traced, and she disappeared.

Could thoughts also make a person disappear? Birdie wondered as she opened her screen door and stepped onto the linoleum floor of her kitchen.

Mathilde Munson stayed after the others left the church basement. She just sat there in the now empty circle of chairs fingering the ribbon in her Bible and thinking of how long she'd known all those women of Bee's age. Since they were born, that's how long. Then first grade through eighth she'd taught them in the one room school house at Common Place. Every one of them, Will and Bud included, had been her students before they graduated to the public school in Greenleaf. You learn a lot about people, both the children and their families, when you teach. Maybe you know them better than they know themselves. She was pretty sure she'd spent more time with those children over the years than their busy parents did. Every day, all day, they sat at their desks looking up at her, all eight grades of them from the little to the big. Eighth grade boys are tall and strong as men and work as hard. It got so she looked UP at Will Fenelon. And looking up AT is nowhere near the same as looking up TO, although with Will, she had to admit to herself, TO and AT were both the way it was.

All of them were part of that little country group they called Common Place. Not a town, really, or even a township (though folks called it that), just a group of families that stuck together like a bramble bush. It was a surprise to be hired as a teacher in their little school as they weren't much for outsiders. But she was plainspoken and she figured they had liked that about her. She kept to reading, writing and arithmetic. In the reading they also learned some history, some famous poems and stories including the ancient myths from most every culture. Many of our present day values came straight out of those stories, a fact most people she knew had never even considered. She wouldn't have her students growing up not knowing about the Greek gods and goddesses, or the Sumerians, Hindus, Celts, Vikings and the rest. Who would want to grow up incapable of appreciating Wagner? American Indian stories she considered a must, the Bible, of course, (which they couldn't study in the Greenleaf Elementary.) Mathilde knew her Bible well enough to pull out a verse from memory every time she saw a need. She'd memorized it as a child in Sunday School at First Presbyterian Church in Greenleaf, and read it daily, like a tonic, all her life. The parents of Common Place grilled her on scripture passages in an entire week of interviews and she never missed a one. This was way back before Bee was born. The children seemed to like her well enough, although liking wasn't even a small fraction of her teaching goals.

She insisted they call her Miss Mathilde at least while they were children and she was their teacher. Later, maybe when they'd married and possibly become her friends, they could leave off the Miss, though she really couldn't imagine it, and truth be told it had never yet happened even once. Besides the Bible passages and by eighth grade even a bit of Shakespeare, she insisted each of them commit to memory the poem "IF" by Rudyard Kipling. Between those three they would have all the wisdom they would need to get themselves through life. Also all the myths, like spice in the educational soup.

Just thinking about all those things gave Mathilde the urge to open the cover of her Bible where she'd inscribed all the words of Kipling's poem and read them to herself again.

If you can keep your head when all about you
Are losing theirs and blaming it on you;
If you can trust yourself when all men doubt you,
But make allowance for their doubting too;
If you can wait and not be tired by waiting,
Or, being lied about, don't deal in lies,
Or, being hated, don't give way to hating,
And yet don't look too good, nor talk too wise;

Widow's Walk

If you can dream—and not make dreams your master;
If you can think—and not make thoughts your aim;
If you can meet with triumph and disaster
And treat those two impostors just the same;
If you can bear to hear the truth you've spoken
Twisted by knaves to make a trap for fools,
Or watch the things you gave your life to broken,
And stoop and build 'em up with worn out tools;

If you can make one heap of all your winnings
And risk it on one turn of pitch-and-toss,
And lose, and start again at your beginnings
And never breathe a word about your loss;
If you can force your heart and nerve and sinew
To serve your turn long after they are gone,
And so hold on when there is nothing in you
Except the Will which says to them: "Hold on";

If you can talk with crowds and keep your virtue,
Or walk with kings—nor lose the common touch;
If neither foes nor loving friends can hurt you;
If all men count with you, but none too much;
If you can fill the unforgiving minute
With sixty seconds' worth of distance run—
Yours is the Earth and everything that's in it,
And—which is more—you'll be a Man, my son!

Oh, but it was good to read it once again and to remember as she read how she'd give each child a line that would be their own for life. She always meant for it to be a kind of gift, something to anchor them in goodness and provide them with something sturdy to hold onto during hard times.

What lines had she given to Bee? To Will? Poor Will, whatever his were he hadn't needed them for all that many years, and she hoped that Bee, wherever she might be, was finding good use for hers. Though maybe she was not. Mathilde had learned over the years that Bee Fenelon's mind leaned less towards the practical and more towards what Mathilde would call philosophical meanderings.

During their Bible study on this day Mathilde had kept her council. She would talk with them about the book of *Exodus,* but not much about her knowledge of Bee Fenelon, Beatrice, her best student in all the years of her teaching career. What a curious mind the girl had, what a unique manner of regarding both people and events. She didn't belong in Common Place, not because anything was wrong with the place or people, but because it was Mathilde's observation that Bee had needed mental stimulation beyond what even a beautiful environment and kind people could offer her. It had been her great hope that Bee would attend college after her graduation, but instead she married Will whose roots were planted so deeply in this land that only death could move him. And as it turned out, not even death could do that, for here he was planted, not just his roots, but every bit of him.

Mathilde hoped Beatrice had finally escaped. She hoped she'd left her crocheting behind inside her house and, by whatever means she could, had found a place where she might fit, where people lived who might appreciate the brilliant gift of her thoughts, of her perspective.

Christin Lore Weber

THE STRANGER'S HOUSE

TRANSPOSITION

MUSIC WAFTS SPACE, hollow as my body's sacred parts, hollow as the God of gods from which flow the worlds. Empty flute of the stranger through which life might return to me. I lay my body on the slate blue tiles at his feet and allow the flute's tones to enter, not as something by which I will be filled, but rather a vibrating field of light in sound by which I can be cleansed and healed of the lingering presence of death.

Is the god of my own imagination flowing through me in the music of the flute? Is it emotion in that tremolo? Or do vibrations of light in the darkness of space, whether womb or mind or immensity of the Not Yet, turn to music as they move? How can I feel what is Not? And yet I do feel. Light weaves through me into sound, and sound slides into the space of every open atom of my being. Not mine. No part of this unmaking can be "mine." Am I even here, on the blue tiles, at the stranger's feet, at the ocean's edge, disappearing? Transposing all of me from widow into song?

Christin Lore Weber

THE STRANGER'S ABSENCE

YOU LEFT ME.

                                    I will never leave.

I woke and you were gone.

                                    I wander
                                    back and forth
                            throughout the world.

I feared you dead.

                            The death you fear
                                    has happened
                                    and is passed.

Death returns
At any time
In many ways
To anyone.
Do you think I do not know?

                                    You do
                                    Not know.
                    What you think you know
                                    Is useless now.

Do not leave.

                            I can never leave.

The husband died.

                            But did he leave?

TOUCH

THE STRANGER puts his flute down on a bamboo stand at his side and reaches to touch my hair, still wet from the waters of the creek.

"You've been swimming."

"In the creek. Pia..."

"Ah. Pia."

"She's like no one else I ever met."

"We all fall in love with Pia."

"Did you?"

"Did you?"

He kneels beside me where I lie on the slate blue floor. "Your dress. It also has been swimming." He lifts it from my body and removes it in what seems a ritual. I feel it like eyelashes everywhere on my skin as he moves it slowly up and over my head, letting it lie as a halo.

"Did the water touch you so?" His voice is a translation of the deep tones on the sea. "I think you and the waters joined; you still are wet."

His tongue on my skin is music.

Inside, outside—music.

The ocean thunders.

Did you and Pia touch?

Our hands;

I held her hand.
Our bodies like fish
Suspended.

> The body is a song
> To be heard
> By whomever is open and awake;
> The body is a beauty
> Not to be squandered.

Pia is beautiful.

> Yes.

She called me Beatricé.

He stands and holding my gaze begins to remove his silk meditation kimono. Naked, he lies beside me and I lift myself to hover over him, my hair caressing him as I move from his face downward. Once I was called plain, I remember as I move. Once no one wanted me. But the stranger...

"You are the beautiful one..." I murmur over and over as my body becomes more sinuous in its movements. He begins the chanting sounds he joins to the act of love. Mesmerizing, musical, hypnotizing. I lose my mind in the movement and the sound. Our bodies dance like wind currents, like currents of water in, out, around, catching the sunlight.

Afterwards he leads me to his bed where we fall asleep, still touching, reaching into and holding one another. "Beatricé," he murmurs as he falls asleep. "Again and again you come to me. My beautiful Beatricé."

VOICE

DURING THE NIGHT, wind begins to blow from the west, billowing the green curtains and setting their bones clacking. I was dreaming of my name, and awake I still can hear it, a child's voice echoing down long empty corridors. My name but more. A multitude of names spiraling into one. That one name I hear as breath emerging from a wooden flute, infinite but particular in each small thing. My name calls from everywhere: each chiseled bit of sand, each shell polished by the constant tides, each stone, each leaf of every tree, each tree itself, each eagle, gull, hawk and cormorant with spread wings, each tufted puffin and storm petrel, all, singing, clucking, setting loose a tone by which we hear the wind, each human voice, every creature's cry. I hear the call in colors indescribable: the peacock's tail, glister of the hummingbird, shimmer of a rainbow trout, never repeated tones of moss in sunlight, glacial blue, ephemeral green, oak brown in the eyes of love.

Christin Lore Weber

I rise from bed to answer the call. By the window I stand and gaze out over the absolute black of the ocean under a silence of stars. Who calls to me? From somewhere or from nowhere comes a verse I somehow once had memorized, or maybe in a different form and time, my own soul was the wheel on which these words were spun. How can I know? I recognize every word, meter, image and line so perfectly, it seems engraved upon my heart.

Rain drew a curtain across the ocean
After our night's dance of love. Each movement
Of the body's music smoothed time
Into an eternal swirl on this cosmic stage
And became a shining path to where
The first note joined the last
In a release of breath that drew us
Through an aperture of stillness vast
Enough to hold the endless tone
Of All.

The Voice, mine and another's, swirls. Like droplets of water each word contains the others while remaining individual. I can see each drop universal. Seeing and hearing, then, becoming one with no difference between eyes and ears. I leave the room to follow, down the stairs and barefoot on the slate blue tile. Am I in a dream? I walk through a door I've not seen before onto the rocks above the surf. Spray collects into droplets on my face and hands. When I look down I see in each drop a world lit up from within, infinitesimal. And in each microcosmic world I recognize among the multitude of forms one form that repeats and repeats, as if in mirrors placed at perfect distance from each other on the walls of time, and the form is the Voice calling out "Beatricé" through the endless light.

Christin Lore Weber

COMMON PLACE

Widow's Walk

BIRDIE

BIRDIE LIKED TO KNIT. Each year at the Craft Fair at the Common Place Church everybody both in Greenleaf and the Common Place would snatch up her afghans and doilies and shawls and caps and mittens and scarves and those handy toaster covers. Bee watched her friend and learned, and once she mastered knitting, she also took up the craft of crochet which, truthfully, she preferred. The friends shared a table at the fair and pretty much sold their entire inventory which meant they'd need to start all over for the year coming up.

Now Birdie kept thinking about all those times she and Bee would get together at one or the other house (depending on whether their husbands were home) and the needles flew and so did the stories and secrets and sometimes the tears. Birdie knew a whole lot about Bee that she'd sworn never to reveal. She had pondered all she knew in the days since Bee vanished and had decided that promises must be kept. Especially in times that worlds seem to be disintegrating, promises become the only safety and stability there is. So Birdie would say nothing; she would knit alone and reminisce.

Bee had been crocheting about a week before she disappeared—that delicate pattern of hers that looked like a snowflake. She'd made about twenty of these in various sizes depending upon the gauge of the yarn—the smallest one you might put underneath a crystal vase, the largest could be a fancy rug. She loved that pattern, the spiral motion of it. She could have done it in her sleep, and certainly had no problem talking while her crochet hook did its circle-dance.

"I've been thinking," she said to Birdie while pulling extra white yarn from the skein (she was making the snowflake into a round baptismal robe for Helen Olson's new baby girl) and kept her eyes on her work as she spoke, "that I probably did love Will." She wound two loops around the hook for a triple crochet. "There was a while there that I questioned it. You remember, Birdie. That time I miscarried and he acted so...I don't know. So nonchalant about it. He was so nonchalant he just seemed cold. Just icy cold." She paused and looked up. "You remember that, don't you Birdie?"

Birdie nodded. She remembered; absolutely she did. She remembered holding Bee in her arms and both of them sobbing. How does a person forget such a thing as that? It's like your womb and your heart are connected and when the blood comes oozing out in gobs, slipping and falling on the linoleum like it did, well it comes from both places. You don't get over that. You just don't, no matter how many years you

live and how many babies you have afterwards. Of
course Bee had none at all that lived. "Oh my gracious
Jesus," Bee had exclaimed, seeing the blood puddle on
the floor between her bare feet, and Will at the kitchen
table waiting for his coffee.

Birdie had gone with her late that afternoon
into the woods. That she would was understood by
each of them without having to put it into words. Bee
insisted they bury as much of the blood as she could
get up from the linoleum in case the baby, tiny as it
must have been, still was lost in those clots. She had
removed her nightgown in the kitchen where she'd
been standing when it happened, and on her hands and
knees, she used her gown. Will walked out as she
scrubbed, as she sobbed and muttered "Jesus, Jesus,
Jesus." Still she bled and allowed herself to bleed,
unable to stop it anyway. And she wiped that up as
well. For an hour, maybe more, she knelt naked, on
her hands and knees, bleeding and wiping until the
gown was soaked and sticky, mixed with blood and
tears.

And afterwards they buried it, Birdie and Bee
together, out among the birches.

"I already loved that baby," Bee had said. "I
really did."

There is nothing like a baby lost, a child whose little life could have reminded you that you had something in you once worth caring for.

KARYN

IF IT HADN'T BEEN for Bee, Karyn Nyström told herself driving home from Bible Study, Will might never have died. Karyn drove exactly at the speed limit, neither faster nor slower, believing as she always had that public rules were made to be kept. If everyone just would follow them there would be no accidents, no surprises, nothing to upset a person's stomach, give headaches, nor, as Shakespeare and Miss Mathilde said, the thousand natural shocks that flesh is heir to. And Bee had been a shock to all of them right from the beginning. Right from first grade at the little Common Place School, and probably before that if truth were told. And how was Karyn to know, living as she did, where she did, scared to death nine-tenths of the time. If Will had possessed the sense God gave a turtle, he would have married Karyn herself, and not that little smarty of a Bee who except for those flashing eyes of hers was downright plain.

Karyn had been pretty. She could see in the bathroom mirror that it was still true. Any boy should have seen the same. But there were rules about pretty. Even Shakespeare knew the rules—"her voice was ever soft and low; an excellent thing in woman." A soft voice came naturally to Karyn. As did a modesty of eyes and dress and movement. She would not flaunt herself, her Swedish blonde hair and what they called satin skin ought to have been sufficient to attract the best of boys. Any boy worthy of her would notice the treasure hidden beneath her reserve. That's what her momma had told her, and it ought to have been true.

If it hadn't been for that Bee.

What a little gentleman Will had been before Bee lit on him and he stuck to her like pollen. Before Bee latched onto him, he'd walk Karyn home from school. Sometimes he held her hand, when he could tell she felt especially shy or nervous about the other children. They were only six years old. He liked her then. He said, "Don't be afraid, Karyn. You're the best of all." Once he held her hand all the way into her house and stood with her in her mother's kitchen. "Mrs. Nyström," he said so politely, "would it be okay with you if I marry Karyn?"

And her mother bent her head a little bit and seemed to think it through. Then she said, "Do you love Karyn, Will?" And he nodded his head so seriously. So she smiled and said, "Well then, when the two of you are eighteen you come back to me and ask again. If you still want to marry Karyn, I'll say yes."

But he married Bee instead.

And Karyn got a stomach ache every time she remembered that. And she got a headache when she thought how he had died way, way too young. And it set her teeth on edge to realize that Bee never really loved him, and Will's death came of knowing that, and mourning that, even though Karyn was right down the road and had loved him all along.

Some folks from the Common Place Church were saying maybe she was raptured, given the way her door was open and her clothes were left along with everything else she owned. But Karyn didn't believe that for one minute. How could someone like Bee be raptured? Someone who'd been given the best gift in the world and was arrogant enough to squander it?

Karyn actually hoped Bee was dead.

This thought caught Karyn up short. It was a serious hope that she wasn't sure she could live with if it were to come true. Could she really hope such a thing? Even if Bee were her worst enemy, which she wasn't, could a person like Karyn spawn such a hope? Across her mind flashed memories of her fears, of times she didn't go somewhere she would have liked, or hadn't said something she believed, or even looked up to meet the eyes of someone she might have liked to know. Wasn't she way too timid for such a hope which she suddenly realized was a form of murder? And anyway, she no longer had a reason to want Bee gone in any of the possible ways she might have disappeared. Will was dead. Neither of them could be married to him anymore.

She was just angry, that was all. She felt she knew things that others didn't about Bee's treatment of Will that made her responsible at least for his illness. And if that were true, then God might be as angry with Bee as Karyn was—killing his beautiful creation like she did—if she did. It really was too much to think about; too complicated to figure out. It was odd, though, how the rules in which you most believe are the very ones you find it necessary to break.

She had reached the turn-off onto her property, the winding road through the woods that led to her house. She felt tired. Maybe she ought to stop attending Bible Study. It really was so draining of her energy to be with those women who couldn't stop themselves from talking about Will and Bee. She'd known them all her life almost, but despite that, something about being with them felt like a weight crushing down on her. She wasn't like She didn't even believe in the Bible. It was a social gathering, that was all. Someone once had told her that it was unhealthy to be a recluse, and she ought to get out among people more. So she had tried.

As she drove up to her house a sense of relief filled her because of the solitude it afforded, the protection.

MARNIE

MARNIE LEFT Bible Study and drove to the Greenleaf clinic where she worked as a receptionist. She knew the business of pretty much everyone in the county. Of course she was sworn to secrecy and wouldn't think of breathing a word, but that didn't stop her from thinking about causes and consequences. Actions and events have repercussions. She'd seen it time and time again.

People appreciated Marnie whose manner was soft as her body and whose comforting words seemed to most everyone to issue forth from the face of an angel. "You're a beautiful, beautiful person." How often had people told her that? Those words gave her a sense of making the world a better place just by being in it—something that warmed her heart.

She'd been at the clinic the day in February when Will Fenelon came in. They engaged in the usual banter that eased the tension anyone feels who is about to find themselves in the examination room. "How'ya doin? / Can't complain. / Planning on planting alfalfa again this spring? / Oh yeah. Thought I might plant in August last year. Glad I didn't with how winter went." Then on to business with the papers to fill out and then the blood pressure and pulse. Marnie filled in with both jobs as much as possible, because such a small clinic can't afford a nurse and doctor both. Because of that she also was the first to know what might be going wrong.

"What will the doctor be seeing you about today?" Marnie had asked Will, according to the prescribed formula.

"Well, Marnie. I have to admit being a little under the weather," he grinned, "nice and gentle though the weather's been lately. Despite those January ice storms, it looks like March will come in like the lamb." He laughed nervously.

She chuckled. She'd always liked Will. Went to school with him all twelve years. "So, Will—where does it hurt?"

"Strange. Can't eat a thing. Can't keep it down, as if I have the flu, but my stomach doesn't hurt; it's the dizziness, I think, that's doing it. Dizziness and nausea. And then there's two of everything. Double vision. And a headache to beat anything I've ever felt.

"How about liquids? Do they stay down?

"Yeah. They do." He grinned. "That's a plus. Right?"

"I sure hope so." She gave him an affectionate pat on the shoulder. "You just sit tight, Will. Doc Johnson will be in really soon."

Being that Will was a man and so was the doctor, Marnie wasn't needed in the room during the actual examination. But on the way out of the clinic Will stopped at her desk to make other appointments with specialists in Fargo, and that pretty much told the story as far as Marnie was concerned. And Will himself looked white as January, which didn't stop him from winking at her when they'd finished with business, or stop her from smiling as usual and calling out "See you soon, Will," as he went out the door. She'd wanted to say "Not good news, Will?" but she knew she shouldn't, and she didn't. And concerning her suspicions, she never told a soul.

MATHILDE

MATHILDE WAS PREPARING to feed her little dog, Prince, whom she secretly held to be the most darling King Charles Spaniel in existence. His actual name was Sweet Prince Hamlet, but she didn't tell anyone because she would have been thought uppity, a characteristic she suspected several people assigned to her anyway. Doctors, clergy, and teachers took care not to flaunt their education in small towns such as Greenleaf where most citizens didn't have that opportunity. She let people believe that she named him Prince because of the breed, and her dog was one step down from being an actual King. That way they wouldn't think she had assumed to associate herself with Shakespeare and other people who might have rather elite tastes. She taught some Shakespeare—that was true. A few sonnets. Some soliloquies. To eighth graders. But really she wasn't a true teacher of Shakespeare. She did aspire to read all of his plays someday, though she'd not been successful up to now. But *Hamlet*! Once she'd seen Richard Burton in the movie, she felt haunted constantly. Of course she had read it in college, in the Shakespeare course she took as part of her degree in humanities. But after the movie she wished she'd driven to Minneapolis the year before the movie came out. She could have seen it live at the grand opening of the Gutherie Theatre, a venue which, at the time, seemed pure fantasy north of Chicago or south of Toronto . She went back to the text, still on her bookshelf from college days, to glean from it in ways that were impossible for her at a younger age. Since then she'd not just read but studied *Hamlet*, memorized parts of *Hamlet,* meditated on *Hamlet,* secretly acted out his soliloquies in front of her bedroom mirror, fallen in love (so to speak) with Prince Hamlet himself. This was not information one could share with anyone from Greenleaf, and certainly not with anyone from Common Place. Naming her dog Prince was enough of a stretch and did raise some eyebrows. And one time Will had seen her walking Prince and asked her point blank if that wasn't one of those royal dogs, the sort the Russian Czars used to have. He'd seen it in a movie about Anastasia. And she'd needed to say yes, because he was right. And English Kings, too. But she didn't say that or anything at all about Hamlet. Let Will discover it for himself.

He couldn't anymore, though, could he? He wouldn't be discovering anything. Unless there were actually a heaven, of which Mathilde wasn't one bit certain despite her daily Bible reading. In fact, she was a severe doubter. But that would be another fact to keep well concealed both in Greenleaf and in Common Place.

She set Prince's dish down on the little rug by the door between the kitchen and the laundry, and went into the living room to read. Every time she entered that room she sighed with relief. It was so... her. Books lined two entire walls in bookcases made of dark walnut. So rich, floor to ceiling. Dutch Arden made them for her when she first returned to Greenleaf after graduating from the university. If she'd had them made now, goodness! They'd be four or five times more pricey. And Dutch had been such a craftsman back in the day. You couldn't find anyone like Dutch around Greenleaf anymore. You had to have been born at the right time. All Mathilde had to do was look at her bookcases to review her entire life. She'd been buying books for as long as she remembered, or people had been giving her books as gifts. Her oldest book was a battered *Mother Goose Rhymes* and it went on from there right up to the latest top of the list of the NY Times Best Sellers. Only the good ones. And by that she meant those on the cover of which the title was larger than the author's name. And it helped if the art were subtle, not gaudy. Also she refused to buy anything written by a ghost writer. It was writing itself that interested her most. Beautiful, well crafted writing done by the same person who had the story or the idea to communicate. Any other way felt deceitful. She inclined towards conservatism in that respect, though she was liberal in almost every other. In this, as in so many ways, she didn't fit in Greenleaf. She would rather not fit than be like the others, though they must not ever discover that.

Christin Lore Weber

The shelves were a riot of color, most of her books first editions in hard covers. She wished they were signed. One time at an antique shop she found a signed edition of a little known, paper-bound Christmas poem by T.S. Eliot! If it had been one of his famous works, like *The Four Quartets*, it would have been worth a fortune. She got it for a dollar and a half, but it was worth a fortune to her. She also had a whole set of classics bound in fine leather of varying colors, and so beautiful she almost didn't want to risk opening them, which was silly, she knew. They came as an offering with her first American Express card. Twenty-five dollars a book. A steal. They included the complete works of Shakespeare bound according to genre. She went straight to the tragedies which opened right to *Hamlet*.

That poor boy, she thought of them all together—Hamlet himself, her little Prince, and even Will who never asked for what he got. But then Will, innocent as he might have been of the relationship between choice and consequence, still did, one might say, sow the wind and reap the whirlwind. Not from Shakespeare, she knew, but from that fiery prophet, Hosea. Her Bible did come in handy as a literary reference if not the eternal promise it was advertised to be.

Widow's Walk

Anyway, poor boys—including Jesus, if one wanted to delve that far into the topic of choice. She traced her index finger down the page. Ah yes. They had a name for what was wrong with Will; however his cancer was but the consequence. Bound within a nut shell that young Will was. She'd known him since his birth. Bounded in a nutshell, like Hamlet, and suffering from bad dreams.

Christin Lore Weber

The Stranger's House

DIFFERENCE

I SEEM always to be waking up. This must mean I also often am asleep. Dreams and life begin to meld and difference eludes me. Always I wake to the pounding of surf and the clicking of the bones. This has become my clue to where I might be. The children I have sometimes glimpsed from the rock play in an endless shine of light, and are silent but for their occasional laughter and sheer high emissions of delight. Which can I be sure is real? The world of silence or of sound? The stranger comes to me with sound.

He comes to me, in fact he wakes me with a touch that flows like the curtains of the room, or else like the underwater kelp. Is he the kelp and not a man at all? The difference eludes me. He is water in which I am immersed. The ocean and the ocean's sound. He is the wet that flows through me like blood or lymph, keeping me alive. I wake to him. I wake in him and he in me. I hear the internal voice of the never-ending as though my ears are sonar, sending signals, charges to the trackless depths.

Deep calls unto deep
at the noise of your waterfalls:
all your waves and billows have gone over me.

-New King James Bible, Psalm 42

101

Who could he be?

Is he somehow the environment for my spirit and my life? Open silence and the rising of sound— is that what I am? Not simply silence. Not only sound. I linger in the silence, falling deeper and deeper, and sound springs forth. If the field of being is a spiral of silent intensity at the core, but spinning out to great and greater inclusion, is the stranger the thread of sound, the echo, that reaches from end to end mightily and orders all things sweetly?

PIA

"DO YOU KNOW who he really is?" I ask Pia when she appears next at my kitchen door. Again she comes as the representative of earth in all earth's colors. Scarves and capes and skirts and veils. She seems the leaves and rain and every form of flower. She moves like cirrus clouds caught in an airstream. Her voice, resonant, combines the call of all creatures of sound, wolves and whales, the canary and the dove, never before heard symphony.

If not for the husband's recent death her voice would amaze me. The presence of the stranger would amaze me. The ocean and the stream and the precipice of rock all would amaze. But I fall backwards, mute

and helpless, into the weave, the incantatory net of
her.

                   If you still need to ask who he is,
               you are not yet able to hear the answer.

But am I safe with him?

                           Has he injured you?

He has not. He has given music;
Life. But I don't know where I am,
Or why.

                          Do we ever know?
                      Perhaps we never know.
                And when we think we know,
             We are farthest from the truth.
                        Let it be.

She runs water in the kettle and makes tea, pouring it
into china cups thin as shells. "The men who walk
with us are and will be many. Tell me about your
husband," she says. "The one who died."
     We take the cups into the scroll room and sit
looking out the large windows at the sea while I try to
explain to her my life in the Before.

Christin Lore Weber

THE HUSBAND BEFORE

HE COMES TO ME in the night. Terrible. Dead. But somehow still alive and pulling on me to be with him, make love to him. He's alone, I think, and cannot be alone. He's afraid to be alone. The awful thing is that I don't know his name—not anymore. Maybe names only mattered before. Maybe he no longer has a name. Maybe he is no one now and doesn't know. Maybe he thinks I can tell him that if he joins himself to me, here, he once again can find his name.

I do remember fragments of what he was before. The husband had eyes the color of spring blue. Into those eyes I could travel just so far before the pathway stopped against a barrier of trees and brambles, growing over stone. He spent his time moving stone, farther, nearer, depending on a whim I couldn't understand. Far or near the stone was always underneath the green so I could never reach his heart. Mornings I would wake to find stones piled on the path to him as though he had spent the night in excavation.

Oh, Pia. Do you think I wanted not to reach his heart? And did he know?

I never reached his heart.

Widow's Walk

When I came close he punished me. A gray cloak covered his eyes, and the husband disappeared into silence.

What can be said? Nothing can be said. He went to the field. I opened a book or picked up my crocheting, or I walked the dusty roads to town. I remember that much: walking the roads and breathing the dust into me until I choked on it.

Each day now he is smaller. I look into the Before and see him there, in the blue field, sunlight on his face, sunlight on the birches, and he is more shadowy. His hands. He lifts his hands to wave and they are almost a woman's hands or else the hands of a child. I can not wave back.

He wasn't always kind. He could fade into a semblance of fog sometimes. When I had no strength to stand and fell him, there was no one there. Where did he go, Pia? Those times? How was I to trust a man who wasn't there? I fell through him then into the brambles; I fell and hit my eyes against stone.

He never raised his hand to strike. He left no evidence. His was the abuse of nothing there. His was the battering we call abandonment.

When we were nine years old we had climbed the massive cottonwood beside the muddy river at the edge of Common Place. He took my hand. The tree had three great trunks, growing into, reaching past and through, making sections we called rooms. He named the tree Trinity after a Catholic belief of his mother's. It was our house. "Pretend that we are married," I told him. I guess I was a bossy sort of girl. He was compliant with me then on the days we sat among the cottonwood leaves and I sang him the very songs my father sang to me. One song was called "Russian Lullaby." I dreamed we would someday live in the music of that song. Freedom. I can't remember why. Were we not already free? We clasped hands, climbing upwards, one room to the next, helping one another.

You loved him then.
I think I did.
Love him.
Then.

CHILD

As evening spreads across the sky I hear the stranger entering. His steps are a rush of stones upon the tide clattering against rock, and over them the light foam of a child's voice. In me the common but mostly imperceptible tremble of life pauses, leaving only the round space of waiting. Into that round she enters.

Do I know her? I can't say for sure that I know her, this waif, this apparition of wide gray pearl, shot through with amber eyes and curls, this little life form, this energy.

I bend to her. "Who are you, little one?"

"Zoë," she laughs, and I think of the Little Prince with his laughter ringing like bells.

WREN

Are you here?

> I am always here
> I look for you among the leaves.

The leaves of letters
That we write. The tones
That tumble from the trees
Of thought.

> I don't know what you mean.

I mean your voice
The way it comes upon me
Here.

> I can't say for sure
> I hear you,

Or that you hear me.

Christin Lore Weber

COMMON PLACE

BIRDIE

BIRDIE MACKENZIE had heard it said that people can die from pure unhappiness, and some said recently that is exactly what happened to Will Fenelon. Well, Birdie said that if he did, it was his own darn fault. If anyone died of unhappiness, it was Bee. If she's dead. Birdie really didn't know that she was dead. But if she were still alive why wouldn't she at least have sent a postcard?

This morning Birdie sat on her porch and thought of Bee. She was knitting, and Bee came to mind. Not that she was ever far from Birdie's mind which runs like a stream, like the muddy river runs through the birches, fast, past the big stones where those two friends used to sit. Birdie never goes there now—not since Bee disappeared. Who could? It was their place of secrets.

They thought their secrets must be different from any other people's secrets still murmuring in the air from the beginning of time. Their secrets could not be told. Whatever they thought might happen if they did tell, Birdie could no longer remember. They were children when they started going to the muddy river's stones, and childhood's a different world. After they were married to Will and Bud the secrets involved happenings stuck in the clay of their daily lives. They still didn't believe anyone else could possibly understand, even though they could see with their own eyes that everyone from Common Place shared the same kind of life. Really, everyone's secrets must have been similar—more or less so, anyway. If they had let themselves see that, they might have felt more free.

Maybe free wasn't what they sought to be. Maybe secretly they clung to that hidden feeling, that closed-in sense, that almost (I don't know) sexual pleasure of planting in each other something improbable. A kind of seed of who they were. A sort of key to the puzzle of themselves.

It's a bit like the crocheting Bee used to do— the snowflake pattern, round and intricate. Orderly, but who could follow it? A maze. A labyrinth. A path around her mind and heart.

Bee never had an orgasm that she didn't bring on herself. Will, she said, could be a wham-bam-thank you-ma'am kind of guy. And that approach didn't help her much, if you know what I mean. He also was a flirt and charming, as every other woman in Common Place and even up in Greenleaf could tell you. Every last one of them was grieving over the loss of him. All promises. All insinuation on Will's part. How beautiful they were, how appealing, what a relief from the wife. Just talk to any one of them. They all blame Bee for snatching him away. As if! If anyone had thought to ask her, Birdie would have said Bee was his safety net, the reason he gave for not bedding any of them down, his cover for inadequacy. And he punished Bee for it. He did.

Birdie never will forgive him.

He drove Bee off, away from Common Place, and Birdie will not forgive him for that.

Bee and Birdie used to sit on the biggest rock above the muddy river, there in the birches, and talk about all this. Year after year they talked. Bee lost her baby, more than that first one, but the others seemed tragedies God sent just for emphasis, while Birdie birthed hers, and they talked. They lived their lives linked to one another's.

KARYN

KARYN RAN to the bathroom and threw up in the sink again. "Oh my God!" she muttered afterwards, gazing at herself in the mirror. "Oh God, now what?" As if she didn't know. She actually did not, not in this part of who she was. Not *this* Karyn. The other Karyn knew, the one who'd been "married" to Will since first grade. The one he really loved.

It wasn't that Karyn didn't know she was lying. It's just that she'd done it all her life. It seemed justified, even required, to create a different form for herself, a good form, stronger somehow, at least not quite so vulnerable, not so shy. The Karyn Fenelon, Will's true wife.

He had come to her for years. She still remembered seeing him walk up her road the first time, not long after her parents died. He'd left his car in the pull off. No one would think a thing of it even if it would be seen. Anyway, it wasn't on her property but on his dad's. He walked up her long gravel road from County 15 connecting Greenleaf and Common Place. More a path than a road, it had become overgrown since her own dad died. It was private by default. She had watched him approach like he was rightness itself coming into her life. Order. Security. A kind of ultimate goodness. At last, she thought, God has set this world on its proper course.

It wasn't as though she thought of him as David and herself as Bathsheba because there was no sin, not like there was for the biblical Bathsheba, because Karyn had never married—not anyone but Will, and that marriage with him predated the other one to Bee. God sanctioned Karyn's bond to him. It was Bee who, even though she didn't know it, sinned. Plus that, for Karyn there was no sex. At least she told

112

herself that although she hadn't been sure and clear for years about where pure love just flowed out through the two of them and sex might have already begun. Did every touch then become an intercourse? Touch couldn't make you pregnant though, and neither could warm breath, wet upon your skin.

Will came to her at least once a week, walking through the long grasses of her road to the front door. He needed her in ways that Bee could not provide. "Sometimes I think that I'm a stranger to Bee," Will had said. "I can't seem to talk to her the way I can to you." She'd never told a soul. Not one soul. "I need you," he said to her. "I've always needed you, Karyn. We're like those children on a broken bridge in the painting at Common Place school. You know the one. The angel is watching over them. They really have no one but each other and the angel." She would sit in the rocking chair where her mother used to sit, and he would kneel beside her and rest his head in her lap. "Comfort me, Karyn." He'd whisper. No one but Will had ever needed such a thing from her. She caressed his hair. She felt his breath through her clothes as though he was breathing her into himself. In the Bible even very holy men had two wives or even more. What was the harm? Karyn gave Will a needed thing that Bee didn't have it in herself to give. She told herself she was a different kind of wife, a wife with a

completely different purpose. Abraham himself had
Sarah and Hagar. Jacob had Rachel and Lia and a
whole bunch of concubines. Then David. He loved
Bathsheba the very best even though he killed to
possess her. But Karyn hadn't killed. Neither had
Will. God wanted this. The purpose hadn't yet been
clear to her, but time would tell. For then, just
knowing she could comfort him was purpose enough.
Just feeling his breath, damp between her thighs, was
a wedding rite enough.

Except for the times Will came to her, Karyn
lived what she thought of as her public life. She was,
she told herself, like a politician or a movie star with a
public and a private life. Often the two lives were very
different. They had to be, didn't they, in order not to
get confused? In her life with Will, she had everything
she'd ever wanted. In her public life she despised the
other women who talked of him in such glowing terms,
and especially she despised Bee who hadn't recognized
the value of what she'd been given and, so far as
Karyn was concerned, had destroyed it through
neglect or worse—had destroyed Will and probably
also herself.

Will came into Karyn's private life where they
sat in the kitchen drinking coffee and talking about
anything at all. Their talk gentled Karyn's heart. He
might reach across and take her hand. He had a way

of looking into her eyes and melting her. It was like they still were six years old except for his breath on her and the quickening it caused.

No one knew. Even though they both lived in Common Place, no one knew. Even up in Greenleaf, no one had a clue.

She reminded herself that she had been naturally beautiful; of course he needed her. Maybe during all those years he *wanted* her in more needful ways than he'd expressed. It wasn't her fault God made her as she was.

But the other part of her, the public part, began to complain to all and sundry how unfair it was that of every young woman around, she was the only one unclaimed. The private Karyn knew, even when the public Karyn railed against the injustice, that she had made it so because of Will and how she was already his most treasured wife, the one he truly loved, the woman most deserving of his intimacy. And those times that she wished Bee dead, she made herself remember that Bee herself was Karyn's best defense against both gossip and the danger (ever present, she supposed, with men) that she might become irrelevant to Will if once she lost her beauty or her increasing willingness to let him claim for himself whatever of her body or her soul he needed or desired.

Sometimes, home alone between his visits, she seemed almost to lose herself, pondering what exactly she was to him. Maybe she'd developed over the years into a kind of minister—or, more a nun. A woman who held his heart in her own heart. Even after years of his visits, she remained a virgin, in her body at least. He'd never seen her naked all those years, nor she him. But her soul was no longer virginal, if it ever had been. No. Into her soul Will had entered a thousand times. Within her soul the two of them turned to liquid fire that intermingled. It was rapture, that was what it was.

That winter, after he found out he was sick, he seemed to need her even more. "I can't let Bee suffer this," he'd murmured, his head on Karyn's lap, his breath... "I tried to tell her right away, but she cut me off. I'll have to tell her soon because I'll need surgery, but tell her without the emotion. It frightens her. She needs me to be strong."

Then the physical forms of love began. All those years love came forth in intimacies that involved eyes gazing into one another's, of gentle words meant to console, of touch that could only be construed as sexual by associations made in the imagination but not shared as such. But that winter...

Snow rolled off his heavy jacket, puffs of rainbow in the kitchen's electric light. He stamped his feet on the rug. "Come see," he reached his hand to her, "get your coat," and led her into the early night of late winter. They stood together under green veils of northern lights, rising, falling, waving across the prairie sky. "It's a blessing on us," she had said. And he: "Yes. And if we only have this time, and if it is short, it will be enough. All we ever needed will be in this time for us."

Later she told herself they'd been caught in the extremities of life and death. Given such extremities mingled with the years of love between them, even a nun might have found herself yielding. But after all, what did it matter how she thought about it? It happened.

Now he was dead. Bee was gone. And Karyn was vomiting into her bathroom sink while asking God, what now?

MARNIE

BIRDIE AND BEE, that's the way it was ever since grade school in Common Place. Always the two of them. Marnie wandered somewhere at the edges, her long braids and pinafores setting her off as different.

117

Also her weight. Pretty as a picture, her mother said, and they're all just jealous of you, dear. And she was, really, with her gentle eyes and sweet disposition. Miss Mathilde said so, too. Often. "The best of the bunch," she said, and Marnie tried to keep it that way.

Back in grade school, Miss Mathilde gave each of her students a line from the poem, "If." Marnie thought of hers every single day, even now. It was the very first line of all, and if the poem hadn't warned against it, she would have given way to the thought that the choice to give it to her made her special in some way. "If you can keep your head when all about you are losing theirs and blaming it on you…" This seemed a task she certainly could accomplish, and it didn't really seem like people blamed their troubles on her, even though she often was the first to know about the pains and tragedies that afflicted them. Sometimes it might look to others as if they were blaming her, the way they reacted right in front of her with their most unguarded selves. Tears or shouting, even cursing coming from the mouths of usually stoic women inclined to condemn those very things in others. She knew enough not to take it personally, and later those very people would come back to thank her for her calm and gentleness at a time they thought they might have gone crazy without it. They said that. And all she'd done was what Miss Mathilde suggested, and

Rudyard Kipling before her. She kept her head. Her entire life had built itself around that line.

Seeing what she saw each day, truth be told, kept her from thoughts of marriage. The emotion of the clinic's reception room felt more than enough. It already felt to her like being married to the whole town.

She knew exactly what happened to Will Fenelon, and so when Bee came into the clinic afterwards, nothing could have surprised her less. Bee trembled that July day like Granny Jarvis who was ninety-six and hadn't been able to write her name for maybe twenty years. And unlike Granny Jarvis, it wasn't just Bee's hands; she trembled all over, like she'd gone outside in January in her birthday suit. Her teeth chattered so she could barely talk.

"I'm so awfully sorry, Bee," Marnie cooed. She had to have been traumatized, finding her husband like that, out among the birches. It was better, though, than cancer. Marnie had to give him that and forgive whatever might need forgiving. "You come sit down in this other room." She didn't want Bee needing to sit among the other folks who already were looking at her with that unmistakable expression people have when watching a tragedy.

She took Bee's blood pressure and her pulse but didn't ask questions. Even the professional inquiries didn't seem properly compassionate. Best to leave all that to the doctor, even though Marnie had known Bee all their lives. She even went through a phase of envying her, plain though she always was. But Bee had something else, something hidden, and it drew people to her as though they hoped to be chosen, but seldom were. Folks referred to it as magnetism, and it seemed to Marnie like a good description. But strange, too. Because when you took Bee apart and laid all the pieces of her out separately, none of them was something you'd be drawn to. Together, though, each piece fit together, and you just had to marvel, "How in the world does she do that?" A person just couldn't stay away from her. It was uncanny. Look at Birdie. And of all people—Will.

That day Bee's pieces were scattered everywhere and Marnie feared for her. Her blood pressure came in at 195 over 110. That was bad. Dangerous.

"You just lie down here for a while." She told her while she raised the back of the table a bit and put a pillow behind Bee's head. "Here's the latest *Redbook*. I just loved the story on page 68. Have you read it yet? It's about a little boy who remembered his second grade teacher all his life. You won't believe what he ended up doing for her!" Bee took the magazine from Marnie's hand. Her voice shook when she thanked her.

"I'll be gone for a few minutes to tell the doctor you're ready. You just relax, okay?"

"Okay, Marnie." Bee said. "I don't know how you do it. So nice all the time."

It was the last she saw of her. The doctor gave her a prescription for some Lorazepam, so Marnie figured the high blood pressure was most likely temporary and the result of grief anxiety. It was hard to see her this way, as though life itself had tricked her into being part of one of those books she was always reading, a drama gone wrong.

MATHILDE

When Mathilde heard that Dickson planned to switch from Shakespeare to the Greeks, and especially that he thought it was a good idea for those Greenleaf High School students— children, really—to present Anouilh's *Antigone*, she walked right down there, into the faculty room, and told him exactly what she thought of that idea. Too immature, she told him. You just cannot lay such profound emotions and philosophies upon the souls of children, even if they are seventeen. Read it—maybe. But *act* it? *Memorize* those lines—some of them at least—why lines like that

will stay forever in the mind. Forever those lines will
affect the outlook, the emotions, the sense of those
children's world. Even without knowing it, those
children for the rest of their lives will reference the
lines they spoke this very year and make their choices
based on them. It's actually dangerous. Mathilde told
herself that she knew all about the classic myths and
how to use them in education. She had done it herself
throughout her entire career. But not like this. Wrong
age. Wrong play. Wrong town. Does Dickson have no
common sense?

It's all there in the first lines the chorus speaks,
the bit of foolishness about the girl knowing she's
about to die and there's no help for it. The very notion
that forces other than human would whirl her right
out of this world simply because of who she was:
Antigone! There could be no choice for her. This was
her fate and she would need to bend to it. Fate. Pure
and simple. Where's free will? And now, for goodness
sake. In a town where Will died and Bee has
disappeared. So young. And giving our children this
fate nonsense, this Greek deterministic philosophy. It's
simply wrong. Is this what we want them to think
happened to Will and Bee? Is this what we want them
to anticipate in their own lives?

Give them Kipling! Give them Shakespeare,
even, where choice is the determining force. Or if

Dickson has to go Greek, then give them Bullfinch and the myths straight up, or better yet the Bible, those Greek letters written by Paul of Tarsus. She knew he'd argue. Where's the theatre in that, he'd say. Well give them the book of *Job* then, and act it out according to Archibald MacLeish.

In a town where everyone knows everybody else, doesn't he realize that even seventeen year olds will see how Bee and Antigone could be compared and found to have motives very much the same?

It was unethical what Dickson had done, and Mathilde told him as much.

He had an argument to match each argument of hers. One would expect as much. So did that tyrant, King Creon, in the play.

Remembering Bee, though, conjured the image of the girl at about Antigone's age or even younger. She'd been that age when she first started visiting Mathilde at home. The books drew her. Those walls of books Mathilde had been collecting all her life. She could almost see Bee standing there, pulling one book off the shelf, opening it with care, touching the pages as though they were alive—an exotic bird resting in the palm of her hand. Her entire demeanor changed as she skimmed the preface, examined the Table of Contents. "Oh, Miss Mathilde," she would say, how I'd love to read this one." And Mathilde would loan it to her, of course, because wasn't that a teacher's greatest pleasure? To find an eager student—eager, intelligent and creative. Beatrice was all of that. She would loan the book and then anticipate the next visit, the opportunity to sit together in Mathilde's living room. She would fix Earl Grey tea in her mother's china teapot and arrange petit-fours on a matching plate, and they would talk about the people and ideas the book contained. This kind of talk virtually never happened in the classroom. She had never met another child like Bee with the keen eye and ear with which she had been gifted. The sensitivity to image and to sound. Almost no one else, even among adults, could read like that. Most didn't realize it was possible.

As the years went on, so did their conversations. The books Bee chose to read became more complex, more literary, more classic. She read the entire world in those books. Naturally Mathilde had expected her to do something with that ability, that sensibility, that knowledge. But she became a farmer's wife. It broke Mathilde's heart.

Was what happened to Bee Mathilde's fault? She wondered that all of a sudden. Once Bee knew the things she knew and had experienced the world the way she had, including the many manifestations of the human soul in its light and shadow, could she again feel at home in Common Place? Was it possible to have seen too much?

It had all started when Mathilde and Bee discussed *Antigone.*

And Mathilde exhaled a shaky breath.

Christin Lore Weber

THE STRANGER'S HOUSE

Widow's Walk

ZOË

UNTIL I COULD SEE her standing on the slate blue tile I didn't know the complete void of childlessness. I didn't know how a child can milk you of a substance you didn't realize you possessed until she needed it. Then in release, in surrender, you become what otherwise you would have never been. I feel no effort in release, just as the exhale of breath is effortless; it is holding back that causes agony. My body bends itself upon one knee, a genuflection. "Where did you come from?"

"I came here on the wind," she says, and from the way her curls are tossed I lean towards believing her. Besides, in her I can't find any opposites. There seems no difference between dark and light or yes and no. It upends me. If I take her seriously will she, at the next moment, break out in that delicious laughter which I love despite (or possibly because of) the way it dizzies me. She seems the Tao awake in a human child's form, seeing the point of light through darkness, and the void within a scintillating gleam.

"But where? Where did you come from?" I reach my hand out to her, but not to touch her. What is it? Respect? Does one need consecrated fingers to be worthy for such touch? Do I need a holy priest to wrap my fingers in silk after anointing them with sacred oil before they can bear contact with such lightning? She is but a child, I tell myself, at the same time knowing my arguments are a ruse against my own intuition.

"I don't know." She laughs as though coming out of nowhere results in penultimate delight, teasing with what might be the adventure of a lifetime.

Greedy, I persist. "Right before here, though, where were you then?"

"In the stranger's hand," she might have laughed again, but she does not. Her little face seems that moment carved in the calm marble of the Pieta, every feeling contained and motionless, but powerful in stillness as the moment just preceding the original Word.

I look up into the stranger's face. He has been watching, engrossed. "I thought the two of you could help each other," he says.

"Is she staying?" I inquire.

"Not long, but for long enough. I hope to teach her the fundamentals of the flute while she's here. She has the capacity for music and it will sustain her when she leaves us and continues on her way."

His way of talking about the child is odd, as though she soon could care for herself. But how could she? She looked to be not more than four years old, though admittedly precocious, or maybe simply enigmatic. Despite those qualities, what person of her age can go on through life alone?

"Will her parents be coming to get her soon?" I ask him.

"Her mother can't care for her right now," he replies. "She's unable yet to return to her. She'll be with us here until she is prepared to leave."

Can't care for her? What could it mean, can't care? I look at her and try to find in her vibrant face something lost or something never having been and restricted from future becoming. Is this something mine or hers? I don't recognize it as my own, but connected to me so intimately that without it I would have no breath, no beating heart.

"Where did you find her?" I wonder aloud.

"It isn't like that," he says. "Do you remember how it was with you? Would "finding you" have been a reasonable description of the moment that we met?"

I see him in what once was my kitchen, a stranger at my table, waiting, as though he'd been there all the time, from the beginning, before the husband, if "before" could even apply to what he was or how he happened to be where he was—wherever he might be. I remember hearing phrases like "frozen in time," or a photographic result called a "still." Perhaps he is still there. My mind tricks me. If he still is there, is he also here? I see him in a glass reflecting through the entirety of life, as though each moment remains eternally, an infinity of stills, gathered. I catch my breath.

He laughs. "You see it," he says.

"Is this the child I saw wandering on the beach?"

He smiles.

"I never told you about her," I say to him. "I thought she might be my own child, but then I couldn't say for sure I'd ever given birth, or if I had, was the child a boy or girl. But it didn't matter to me then. Just to see the child in the mists, holding the husband's hand, sufficed to fill the flowing parts of me with hope. But they disappeared. I might have heard the child laughing as they faded from sight. The hint of her existence..."

"Is enough."

Are we all reflections, I want to ask, but even as the words rise in me I am aware they are not adequate. Light passes through the glass, but does it not also reflect? And the glass itself is only a manner of speaking. The bird sees itself in the window, as though the glass has become a mirror, and depending on its urgency it flutters against the solid pane, or in a flurry of desire, crashes there and dies. Are we reflections in a drop of penetrable rain, then? Or in the molecules that make up air? And if we are reflections what being does each of us reflect?

When I take Zoë's hand she feels solid as anybody I have ever known. "I know a hawk who rides upon the currents of the sky as if air is solid underneath her wings," I say to her. "Shall we go outside to find her so I can introduce the two of you?"

Her small hand in my larger one is a promise I never thought would be fulfilled.

BEES

A SWARM OF BEES inhabits the giant oak where the path enters the woods. I recognize their voices, the buzzing hum of their swarm, as though I am somehow one of them and with only a small turn of mind I could remember their language. I take Zoë there.

"Can you understand what they are saying?" I ask her. She is transfixed. It is mid-afternoon and they are flying in and out of the tree, carrying their loads of nectar I would suppose. Is it with their wings they speak? I remember from somewhere that they dance their message, creating a map of heavily endowed flowers. Zoe watches them and listens.

"They sing about a field of lavender," she says. "I've never seen a field of lavender. Could we follow them?"

"Would we need wings?" I wonder how far away this field might be. I'm already believing her; why would I not? Already I can see myself dancing in the lavender like an actual bee, gathering pollen which becomes a veil that covers me completely.

"But we have wings already," she cries out, spreading her arms and whirling on the path. A bee settles on her arm. "Oh," she says, "Hello. You silly bee. Don't you have work to do?" She's not a bit afraid. "Your friends are calling you."

I hear them. How is it that I hear them? Bee, they cry, Bee, as though it is my name. But then in a way it is. "Can I call you Bee?" Zoë asks as though reading my thoughts. The thought of it delights me, but I don't know why. "I'd like that very much," I tell her. "It will be my special name because it is a gift from you."

"Thank you, Bee, for taking me to visit your friends," Zoë calls over her shoulder as she dances farther down the path. "We'll come back here lots. Okay?"

"Okay," I laugh and follow her. It seems that behind us from the bee-tree I hear human voices calling my new name.

Widow's Walk

BEATRICÉ

ZOË IS ASLEEP. The stranger and I lie awake. Our voices murmur in patterns of sound like colors in a tapestry, understood by intuition, a language form that appeals to every sense. Its complex meaning relies upon simultaneous sensitivity to variations in light, touch, sound, flavor, temperature, in telescoping dimensions. Imagine if you can. He wakens me beyond the boundaries of myself. I expand to meet his touch. My body is a density within an atmosphere that whirls with such speed that he could touch me from another galaxy and I would quicken. How does he do this? We are silent but I hear the atoms of our flesh as music. I watch as we pass through each other's bodies as I once was told Jesus passed through the locked doors of an upper room. In a way I do not understand, the laws of earth lift when the stranger speaks my name.

WREN

I FILLED a planter with soil
And scattered daisy seeds
On the side of the house protected
From the wind. A little bird
Eats some of them and sings afterwards

Christin Lore Weber

Perched on the planter edge.
Is it you?

I still walk along the road.
I still sing.

It is a wren
Lifting her head to the blue sky
Opening her beak to release the song
The music continues even after
Her beak is closed.
I am entranced by this.

An echo
Maybe.

I don't know.

The song of earth.

COMMON PLACE

Christin Lore Weber

BIRDIE

BIRDIE WENT BACK AND FORTH in her mind when it
came to her life in Common Place. If it weren't for Bud
and the way he fit into the whole pattern of living
there, then all the rules for how everything and
every*one* had their own place exactly, might have
prompted her to leave. Like Bee left. Sometimes she
felt downright angry with Bee for doing that and not
taking her along. How could she just go away alone,
leaving her best friend to cope with what was left?
Sure, she still sang—what else could she do?

You'd think that Bee at least would write.
Birdie checked the mailbox every day, still hoping.

It was getting on towards Fall, though, and
still not a word, not a postcard, nothing. The alfalfa
was plowed under and the birches were turning bright
yellow. Sometimes Birdie stopped in the road right by
Bee's old house and pretended that if she went up the
driveway her friend would come running out the
kitchen door and meet her halfway. On the day she
noticed the birches had begun to turn, she actually did
that. She walked all the way to the porch of the empty
house and sat on the top step. The white paint on the
railing had begun to peel. Will used to keep it so nice,
clean and simple as if he'd been Amish. Truth be told,
he wasn't far from being of that persuasion—a few

generations on his dad's side is all. Some of the habits must have come down in the family and were probably welcomed by his mother's Catholic soul. Few people knew about that part of Will, but though Birdie didn't know much about the Amish or the Catholic way of life, she did think there might be a connection between Will's carefulness about his things, tools and house and so forth, plus his carefulness about rules and keeping things and people in their rightful place, and his devotion to the Common Place way of life. Come to think of it, that way of life resembled the Amish.

She paused in her thinking. Maybe not. What did she know about the Amish, she told herself again. She was leaning on stereotypes, she scolded, and what would Miss Mathilde say about that? Miss Mathilde warned them all about such false thinking that led to dangerous conclusions. Birdie guessed that her teacher had worried about such things more when it came to her than the others. Hadn't she given her a line from "IF" that warned her about all her speculating? "If you can dream—and not make dreams your master;/ If you can think—and not make thoughts your aim…" She'd been working on it and on rare occasions she thought it was good advice. But more than not the notion angered her. She knew she was a dreamer, and she loved that about herself. And figuring things out, her thoughts, they really often did become her aim.

Once she'd figured something out, that seemed the end of it—no need to act on it. That's when Miss Mathilde's advice from Kipling came back to her with a voice of authority. And that's why Bee was so good for her because with Bee if something needed doing Bee and Birdie did it. They didn't just think about it. Birdie took it up like something alive that was injured and needed saving. When Bee was with her, Birdie understood why she'd been born into this world.

She ran her finger over the peeling paint. A chip detached itself and she flicked it off the railing to the weeds that grew where Bee's flowers used to be.

Without Bee there in that house, without her to listen to Birdie's complaints about Bud, without the two of them turning really painful events into humorous parodies, Birdie wasn't sure she could continue to live in Common Place. But then, she was stuck, wasn't she? It wasn't just Bud, and if push came to shove, he could make it on his own, he could do just fine without her, but the children. She couldn't take them with her and she couldn't leave them here. She didn't want to break up the family anyhow. She loved Bud and she loved the kids. But, face it! Bud wasn't enough for her, and she didn't have the wherewithal to support three children on her own. But anyway, without Bee? Impossible. Either option wouldn't work out. A woman needs her friend. She sighed. There she went—thinking again and doing nothing!

Marnie had moved to Greenleaf. You can do that if you're single. If you have a job in town. Even if you belong to the little Common Place church, you're freer, and you're also freer if there's no man watching your every move. She felt a shot of guilt through her entire body as her mind composed that thought, because it implicated Bud, she knew, and she loved him despite everything. But he did watch her. Please God, be merciful to both of them. But he did. And why? What did he think he'd see? He'd see nothing; there was nothing to see.

And this also bothered her. What was she if there was nothing there to see? Nothing there. Bee always saw something Bud had no eyes for, even if he might be looking straight at her, he could not have seen it, not in a million years. Maybe it was the dream in her.

She flicked another chip of paint. And now he wouldn't even if he could. Bee took that part with her when she left. Birdie wasn't clear on how this worked, how a part of you doesn't exist until it is seen from the outside by a friend with sight keen enough to notice it.

Maybe there would be a card in the box today.

Birdie got up from the steps and went back out to the road. She'd check the mailbox first thing when she got home. As she walked she began to sing again, "Always On My Mind," sounding so much like Brenda Lee, and as she sang she didn't know if she meant the song for Bud or Bee.

KARYN

OH LORD. She was pregnant. Well, she couldn't go to the clinic, that was for sure, because Marnie was there and she'd know immediately. She couldn't go anywhere! How could she even leave the house. Damn! Damndamndamndamn. Damn that damn Will, going off and dying like he did. And damn his crazy wife, Bee, who disappeared. And damn all the people in this damn small town and that insane church out at Common Place. And this old house that was too hot in summer and too cold in winter which was not so far off. What in the world was she going to do? And Karyn began to cry.

She cried until she couldn't breathe; then she went into the bathroom and splashed cold water on her face.

She stumbled into the living room and sat on the rocker. This was where it started, only two months before Will died. This was where their love changed. It had started innocently, the way their meetings always

140

proceeded. They'd had coffee at the kitchen table, begun to talk, continued to the delicious gazing into one another's eyes. She already knew, of course, that he was sick, and her eyes began to brim with tears. He reached his hand across the table and with his index finger wiped the tear. "Shhhh…" he said and smiled. Then he took her hand and led her to the living room where she sat, as always, in the rocker, and he knelt beside her, lowering his head to her lap. "Shhh," he whispered again, "it will be alright."

"How will it be alright?" she replied, her voice catching on the words like a burr on fleece.

"Shhh," he said low. She felt his breath warming between her legs. She felt wet, as though her whole body had begun to weep. "Oh, Will," she groaned.

His breathing became heavier. His right hand reached up under her skirt, softly against her thighs, more gentle than anything she'd ever known against her skin, and then his finger slipped into the wet.

She'd suspected for almost five months what was going on because all the signs were there, but for some dumb reason she kept telling herself that maybe she had cancer. What a fool! Who would rather have cancer than a baby? She lifted her head and saw herself in the mirror. Good God! She hated herself so bad. How could she ever have thought she was pretty? She was ugly and she was dumb. And she began to cry again.

There was no explaining it away any more. That baby was growing and moving. She'd woken up in the middle of last night with her mind going a hundred miles an hour trying to figure out how to get herself out of town to somewhere safe. She had a cousin in El Paso. Maybe she could go there. If Bee could disappear, why not Karyn? She barely knew her cousin, but she was family, so they had to take her in. So she could see El Paso. That could work. Maybe.

How in the world could she get herself to El Paso? She'd been living from pay check to pay check with nothing to spare—living cheap and lying to folks about how she didn't need a thing. How she could take care of herself. And then, Will used to give her money every time he came to her place. "Get yourself something pretty, Karyn," he'd say. And she'd use it for necessities. She barely made a thing at work, a nothing job in Greenleaf at the five and dime. But she hadn't gone in for two weeks. She'd called in sick. And now what could she do? Hide out in her house? Live off the garden veggies she'd put up? People might start coming around. The others at Bible Study would miss her, begin to wonder. They'd knock on her door, and there she'd be, big as a house. Oh God! All of them, every single one, thought she was such a good person, shy, fragile, couldn't hurt a fly, would never do a bad thing. And there she'd be.

She could claim to have been raped. This suddenly occurred to her. When they asked why she didn't call the sheriff, she could blush and lower her head and look to the side and her tears would trickle down her cheeks and they would remember how awfully shy she was. She could go on with the story if they asked: how this strange fellow followed her home several times, watching, discovering she lived alone, how he broke in, how terrified she'd been, how she couldn't remember how he looked except for dirty, face a mass of whiskers.

People would believe that story while no one— not one person in the whole county would believe she'd had a love affair with Will Fenelon. And that story of being married back when both of them were in first grade. People would shake their heads and think she'd gone stark raving mad after her mom and dad died and left her with the farm. At least she had a house. At least it was secluded if she decided she needed just to hide. Because how could she get herself to El Paso? She just couldn't. She was scared to go as far as Moorhead. She'd never been there. Fargo neither.

Maybe she could get rid of it now that she was certain it was there, inside her. She'd heard there were ways but she hadn't really paid attention. She'd read novels, too, but they left details to the imagination. You were supposed to imagine how you might use a coat hanger to get inside yourself and dislodge that tiny baby. The images she'd thought up were not possible for her and maybe not for anyone. Women died trying. She'd heard that somewhere, too. Anyway the baby was too big now for a coat hanger to work; she was pretty sure of that.

All these years, every week that Will came to visit her and she made up stories, trying to believe it was normal and right. Not just stories about being a nun for him, but also about how he was her true husband, and he had a trucking route that took him all over the United States. She never included a chapter about getting pregnant. He'd leave late in the afternoon and drive to where his semi was parked and then he'd leave for New Mexico or Kentucky or Oregon with a load of something or other. He'd be gone a week or two before he'd be with her again. It was her story. She'd imagine him in truck stops, eating big breakfasts of eggs and hash-browns, bacon and toast, and drinking enormous mugs of coffee, and telling the other drivers about his sweet wife back home who would do anything, anything at all, for him. And they'd say how they'd love to have a woman just like his. And all this time she never thought of babies as even remotely connected to what the two of them did together. Babies never even came to mind. Also she kept from herself that he actually was just down the road at his own farm, tilling his alfalfa, living with their classmate, Bee, and carrying on as if he didn't even remember Karyn existed.

Now he was dead, and Karyn had his only child inside her body, and Bee who never had his child at all was gone.

Where was Bee anyhow? It suddenly had occurred to Karyn that Bee might actually want to have Will's baby. She knew from talk at Bible Study that she'd tried and even conceived, but miscarried. What if Bee would be willing to pretend that she'd left not only because Will died, but because she was pregnant with his son or daughter? If Karyn could find her, somehow, then they could stay together until the baby was born, then both of them could come back to Common Place, Bee as mother of the baby, and Karyn as, well, what she'd always been.

MARNIE

MARNIE HAD STARTED waking up at four in the morning after fitful nights of dreams and what seemed the voices of townspeople calling out to her from the darkness. Way too often she was making coffee in those hours when her neighbors either enjoyed the coziness of slow waking, even of turning to a partner in the bed and snuggling into another body, trusted, safe; or else were aching with pains both fleshly and spiritual, sunk in an artificial drugged sleep she knew about because she'd seen the prescriptions. She'd witnessed too much suffering, taken too many people into her arms, absorbed too many sobs, felt too much human trembling. Life troubled her.

"You might consider a different job," Pastor Joseph suggested when she sought his counsel. He must know how it feels to be permitted a glimpse into the souls of pretty much everyone in the county. She had asked him how he could bear it, all the loss, all the disappointments, the fear of illness, of old age, the disintegration of the body and the mind. Certainly he'd seen others brought very low. And what about the sheer mystery of it that they all had seen in the tragic death of Will Fenelon and the disappearance of his wife, Bee. "The Lord is merciful," he'd said. "You have to have the calling," he also said, "and the ability to be objective about it all—the Lord gives each person the life most perfectly suited to their needs, every lesson exquisitely designed with its balance of joy and pain, to bring them through this earthly life and into the joys of heaven. We learn to comfort others while not dishonoring them by taking on their suffering as though it were our own. It is not our own. It is not designed for anyone but them."

She couldn't see it. Didn't the Bible say "Laugh with those who laugh; weep with those who weep?" And also, "Bear one another's sufferings." She knew her scriptures.

"You are a secretary, Marnie, not a counselor or a nurse. Mind your calling." He had put his hand on her shoulder in an effort, she supposed, to comfort her. But there was no comfort in his words.

Maybe he was right, though. Maybe she depended on all the emotion she felt to prove the depth of life. Maybe she needed other people's suffering to move her own heart, to bring out her compassion, to give her a sense of being worthwhile. Maybe she needed the voices that called out to her in the night in order that she might know she was part of something larger than herself, needed by the people, as though everyone who came through the doors of the clinic was a member of her own family. And maybe such dependence on the suffering of others, and of course their joy as well because there was that too, was a form of selfishness, a kind of theft.

Maybe she was addicted to it, had to have it like a drug that compensated for (dare she even think it?) the curse of being human.

Christin Lore Weber

"Have faith," Pastor Joseph had smiled. "Just have faith, Marnie. We needn't do great things; a little thing is plenty. God loves you no matter what you do. It really is not your place to bear the sufferings of the whole world, you know. That's been done—once for all, as the Bible tells us. Just be the best little secretary you can be and let God take care of the rest."

She had left the church feeling angrier than she ever had felt before.

Of all the people her age in Greenleaf or the Common Place, Marnie had been the most devoted to Bible teachings and the love of the good savior, Jesus. She realized early in her life that people had their own ways of believing. Some liked to argue over what was right and wrong, and some of those looked for verses from the Bible to support whatever they took it in their minds for what they preferred to do. She didn't hold with that way. Some others just used church gatherings as a social function, and that was okay, but she felt the need for something more than that. Even as a child too young yet for school she had the notion (who can tell how she came to experience this) that Jesus was a playmate. Maybe she was a bit like those children who, because they spend too much time alone, create an imaginary friend. Looking back, Jesus was that friend to her. Looking back, it seemed as though she'd actually seen him, talked with him, run into the woods with him, heard him sing to her as she went to sleep, called back and forth with him down at the wooden bridge that crossed the creek by the church in Common Place.

As a teen she fell in love with him. By then she no longer actually saw him as in a body, but she did feel him so close to her that he distracted her from most other things and people in her life. She spent many afternoons after school by herself in the fields or by the stand of birches, just gazing at the clouds or the light playing off the dancing birch leaves. She was not really alone but rather like someone sitting beside the one she loved. Sometimes she wished she could have been born a Catholic girl so she could marry Jesus as some of them, it was said, were called to do. She promised Jesus so much back then. In fact she promised him everything she had and was and could ever be. "Don't let me ever leave your side," she said to him over and over. He was her beloved.

Why couldn't it be that she now was finding him everywhere in everyone. Why couldn't it be that because she had never left his side, she could see into people just the same as he could? Why couldn't it be that she could feel what he could feel—the same love, the same compassion, the same suffering? And even if she only was a secretary and not a doctor or a nurse or

Christin Lore Weber

even a pastor, why couldn't it be that standing by the side of Jesus and loving without boundaries or distinctions was and always had been the life to which she had been called and given everything she needed to fulfill?

So when the voices woke her early in the deepest dark before morning came, and when the nightmares showed her the most profound terrors of humanity, and when her heart felt stricken with both loneliness and love and the need to comfort anyone who stood in front of her, well, she would let it be. She would not leave the beloved. And she would meet him everywhere.

MATHILDE

DICKSON MIGHT HAVE PONDERED the *Antigone* presentation over the summer, but decided on it anyway. Practice had begun at the beginning of the Fall semester. As Prince Hamlet put Mathilde in mind of Will, brave Antigone never failed to bring poor missing Bee, the thought of her that wouldn't go away, visiting her old teacher's dreams.

One morning towards the end of September she woke from a particularly brutal dream about her former student, and maybe also about Antigone, because it took place in a cave in which Bee was trapped. Still alive she was crying out in a voice that echoed off the stone walls, emerging nowhere that it could be heard. "Where am I?" the captive kept repeating. "Where?"

Mathilde woke shaking. Was the girl actually calling to her? Did she have some responsibility here?

She threw back the covers; it was chilly now at night, and she'd already changed the bed clothes to flannel and the thick quilt old Granny Jarvis made for her those many years before. She grabbed her woolen robe and slipped her feet into the boiled wool slippers always positioned exactly so her feet would not encounter the cold oak floor.

At the foot of her bed stood the spacious wooden chest that had been her mother's, and in which she kept the most memorable documents from her teaching life. She'd kept some things of Bee's; she felt quite sure of it.

So many students. Here were their pictures, papers they had written, poems, cards to her—some of them made with crayon and misspelled words. Of course she would have kept such treasures. But now was not the time to sink into nostalgia. Bee was calling to her.

She lifted out of the chest a metal file and set it on her dresser. Opening it she fingered her way through the manila folders until she came to the one for Beatrice "Bee" Breault. She experienced a flash of indignation. Why did parents do that? Alliterate their children's names. Her own parents had done the same and she'd hated it all her life. She shook her head as if to shake the thought away.

Slowly she turned the pages of Bee's thoughts, the little essays she'd written over the eight years Mathilde was her teacher. There might well be a hint in these, even if the girl was so young when she wrote them. Her teacher's eye picked up the slight variations in penmanship as the girl had developed finer motor control which by eighth grade became a stylistic flare. She was that way, wasn't she? Mathilde thought. Such a flare for life she had.

Then suddenly an essay title nearly made her drop the lined notebook paper right onto the floor. But there it was.

"I Want Everything of Life: My Book Report
On ANTIGONE by Jean Anouilh."

Though Mathilde hadn't assigned the play, it was one of those books Bee had borrowed from her personal collection. She'd given her an "A." Heavens! But well, of course she would reward a student who had tackled such a difficult piece of work. Difficult for a child, that is. Difficult, actually, at different levels for minds of any age. The drama's conflicts took on deeper meanings as cognitive functions became more complex. She held the report in her hand, her heart beating wildly for a person her age. What had the girl seen in it? Mathilde felt on the verge of discovering the seed thoughts, the motivations for Bee's disappearance. She recognized the line in her title as coming towards the end of the play. Mathilde had also been struck by that line when she first read the work. She'd been older, of course—in her late twenties. Still it was like lightning in her heart. The girl, Antigone, a teenager like Bee, confronted with a moral choice of ultimate significance—giving her life in the service of freedom and incorruptibility, even if she could see no earthly benefit for her sacrifice. An irony, wasn't it?

"I want everything of life." Such a...such a *young* declaration. Maybe this was Mathilde's problem with having young people act myths and other stories out on stage. What if they believed it? Well, of course they would believe it. Why else do the boys go to war than their belief in it. Why do girls sacrifice themselves? Like Antigone many would choose freedom over moderation and compromise, even if the cost of their freedom would be their own death. Bee's essay was three pages long, written large, with pencil.

Mathilde picked it up from the floor, sat on the edge of her bed and began to read.

I Want Everything of Life
A Report Based on the Play
"Antigone"

Beatrice Breault

Antigone is my heroine. From the beginning of the play, I recognized her. She could have been my sister, or even my twin, the way she held back against her fear and remained strong even when threatened with death. She remained true to her beliefs and never betrayed herself or the brother she loved. We all love to be alive, and it can feel like a betrayal to the world and people we love when we make a choice for sacrifice in the interests of justice.

It is hard to experience opposite desires. That is what Antigone required of herself. She says she wants everything of life and wants it now. But at the same time she makes the decision to sacrifice that life she wants in order to bury her brother, Polynices, in obedience to the will of the gods, and to assure his safe passage to the land of the dead. She refused to compromise. She refused to be moderate. I wonder if I could be that brave. Her Uncle Creon, the king, had

154

her buried alive in a cave as a punishment for burying Polynices. But she took life in her own hands and hanged herself in sacrifice.

Would I have the courage to do that? I don't know.

I'm often afraid. Sometimes I lie. So who knows? I might be the sort of person who couldn't even be chosen by Antigone for a friend. But I do feel a lot like her when she said she wanted life now. I do too. I want all of life just crammed into this very minute.

Miss Mathilde gave me an IF line that I thought was too hard for me. It might have fit Antigone though. *If you can watch the things you gave your life to broken, /And stoop and build 'em up with worn out tools…* But me, I want all of life and I want it now and not to have to fix it. Not to have it broken, ever. Antigone did both. But I honestly don't think I could. That's why she's my heroine.

Mathilde sat staring at Bee's essay. Good Lord! That poor girl. She noticed that her own hand was trembling. It was as though she'd been a prophet when she handed out those lines. Maybe a person ought not do something like that. Talk about giving suggestions to young minds—she'd done the very thing she'd been railing against. If anyone's life had been broken it was

Beatrice Breault Fenelon's. And she never did pick it up so far as Mathilde was aware—not with worn out tools nor with any tools at all.

THE STRANGER'S HOUSE

Christin Lore Weber

TO WREN

SOMETHING IS WRONG here. I'm not sure where I am,
or even *IF* I am. Where are the connecting points?
Did I send letters to you? Cards? I can't remember
mailing them. And did you write to me? If you did,
where are the cards? Surely I would have saved them,
but I've searched the entire house. In the bedroom
there's a small chest made of some fragrant wood. It
looks to have been Asian made with carvings of
dragons and a unique brass lock. I think I would have
kept your letters to me there, but when I looked, I
found it empty. I searched in cabinets and drawers in
every room that contain such things. But there is
nothing even of my own. Doesn't that seem strange?

Things happen to me here and all of them seem
real. The places, surely they are real. I touch them;
they are solid. The rain is wet. The ocean spray is salty
on my tongue. I taste the wine and hear the flute and
feel the stranger's touch. The stream flows over the
rocks and Pia's voice and touch are actual. But what
sort of place is it that consists of four people? In all
this time I've met only the stranger who seems to have
no name, and Pia whom I love as dearly as I love you,
and a child named Zoë. With me that equals four. The
path goes to the stream in the woods, down to the

158

ocean, over and back to the stranger's house. A triangular enclosure. Is there a beyond?

It is as though I am in a dream with a series of vignettes unconnected. Each of them is surrounded not by a boundary of any sort—not a wall, not a veil—but by endlessness. The deer travels the path. The hawk flies overhead. My name floats towards me on the wind.

If you get this, Wren, please try to reach out to me somehow.

RAIN

I FIND MYSELF ALONE in the house as rain is falling. Day and night I am alone. The rain is never ceasing, changing everything. At first I search for the stranger, then the child, but I think they have gone off again together. How could it be I would catch but a glimpse of her, of Zoë, before she would be taken, and with the taking would also leave but traces of the stranger? His flute is here, in the scroll room where the large windows stream continually, softening the outside colors to mute tones. What can I do but watch? Beneath each shift of the spectrum a glide of gray, the ambient ghost of light, liminal, as at twilight when color disappears, or pre-dawn when one recognizes outlines and that is all. Then the wash, as though an artist, slowly carefully, let the water flow over a Sumi painting of a cove with ruined trees emerging through wet atmosphere.

The fog horn on the buoy by submerged rocks mourns.

Why would I be brought here if only to be left alone?

This rain is without wind, a calmness of weeping such as seldom overcomes a person or a world. In the particulate I stand, looking out on nothing but a flow of being, unheeding myself as a continuation of that flow, tears like the very essence of me, a condensation of spirit taking form with no sense yet of being separate.

So barely here.

I wear the silk kimono of the stranger, that in which he wraps his body each morning when he steps out onto the deck above the ocean to pay homage to the light. He does this in silence before the first clear sound of the flute. I do not go onto the deck. I do not step into the rain. I do not see the light. I do not blow the air from my lungs into the flute.

What is this silence? What is this stillness into which I've come? The stillness of this rain?

Widow's Walk

It seems I once heard of a tribe that sent one person out to stand on a cliff in the darkness before the first ray of light each morning. His presence there and the song he sang made the sun rise. Without him darkness would engulf the earth. The world would end. Do I now stand on that edge?

MEMORY

THE RAIN continues to fall, in darkness, in the between light. I continue alone. What were called days have passed, not seeming to pass, all as the rain that continues. I remember even less of the Before. This interruption of memory had been a form of relief, but has now become a form of loss. Yet there is no time upon which to measure this passage.

The thought to capture memory fragments comes to me upon leaving the stranger's house to feel the rain's intention. Long grasses grow along the creek side. I walk there, bare feet upon the path, in the mud that forms as rain mixes with earth. Red grasses grow in clusters. The green have tassels that in dry times blow in wind as one light whisper on the hill. In rain the tassels hang like fairy hair draped towards the ground. I pick an armful of them and sit on the rock where Pia and I came to know each other. There I

begin to weave. In the weaving a memory begins to
form of holding a silver hook and forming a snowflake
by pulling loops of thread one through another,
creating finely crafted knots. It had a name. Crochet.
The wet grass now bends easily, braiding,
intertwining, and my fingers seem instinctive towards
the craft. A wren was a little bird, I think as I weave,
in the Before.

Back in the stranger's house, now seeming like
a giant rock balanced above the ocean, I go directly to
the bedroom. On the table beside the bed lies a book
that I haven't seen before. How had it come to be
there when I had been the only one to enter or exit the
house? Had someone come while I sat by the creek-
side in the rain? I take it into my hands.

Hands crafted this book, the cover linen, woven
on a delicate loom and collaged with handmade paper
in which can still be seen fragile bits of grass turned
golden, flower petals, and traces of moss. Affixed to
the cover's center is a metal ornament, also hand done,
brass, I think, or maybe copper because it holds a
spray of green, such as copper turns with age. And
beneath the ornament which includes a gold spiral of
existence, is written by hand *Get lost in your passion.*

The handmade paper pages of the book's
interior are blank.

Widow's Walk

Beside the book, a pen. Beside the pen a pot of ink. I dip the pen. I smooth the first page, and at the top I write:

Remember

She's driving west and yellow leaves drift by the car, by the windshield—tarnished leaves of the birch tree. She's driving west towards Jamestown on the new highway through fields on either side, and wondering small things about him like will he sleep the whole night through or will he wake sometimes and lie there wondering? Will he lie there between clean white sheets, smooth sheets, slick like silk, but not silk, of course, but cotton—and will he wonder as she wonders if there might be a God after all who has the power to condemn. She's driving west along the new highway, past the quaint towns, towards the city, wondering about him and whether he can sleep at night. Her mind drifts like a birch leaf, tarnished yellow and brittle in the afternoon sun.

I put down the pen and wonder who "she" is. She seems a woman in memory. Myself? But how is that possible? And who is the "he" inside the wonder of the woman's mind? Is this memory? I'm almost certain it is and that memories will increase again now that I'm alone wherever I am and whatever this place is.

The stranger still has not returned.

Night, and a great wind. The groaning of trees on the cliff's edge. I am weary. I cried today because passion is gone. I feel, suddenly, nothing. And yet I cry. Is that not passion? I fall into it, now, again. Now I cannot stop. I am the weeping. I am the tears, the rain. The loss. This is the grief, and it, at least, remains. The loss remains.

Did the husband really die? Or was it God who disappeared?

I could go back, she thinks the next day when a branch whipped and snapped her in the face. The long lash of it, the red welt, brought tears, as though small as it was, it contained the insult of everything that had been done to her—everything lost, taken really. She reached out her hand to touch her face. There was no blood.

She is lying on the dry leaves, underneath the tree. The tears, all of them, have now been cried.

RETURN OF THE STRANGER

I HEAR HIM on the threshold. The child is not with him. I would have recognized her steps. She would have laughed. Perhaps called out. In a dream she asked if she could call me Mama. But I was not sure, even though that word, that—name, had been my everlasting longing. One must not assume, because who is it bestows a name? Immediately I wanted to ask him where she was and wherever that might be, had he taken her there and if so, why? Didn't I need her? Didn't she need me? Hadn't he said as much?

He comes in through the bedroom door. "Come out," he calls.

I'd taken refuge behind the green curtain. How long I had been crouching there I can't know. A moment. Years. I need concealment. I am a secret; I realize that now. I am a secret who does not know what she contains. The passing is in an eternal clicking of the bones.

"Why did you take her away?" I whisper and the thick fabric of green mutes my words, but he hears me anyway.

"She is not yours to keep." His voice is tidal. It is blood-flow. It is underground rivers. "Did you never read Gibran? 'Our children are not our children. They are the sons and daughters of Life's yearning for itself.'"

"Is that who you are? The taker of what we will not give?" My voice has the sharp edge of accusation. I hate him for leaving. I hate him for taking. I hate him for trapping me in this triangle of aloneness. I hate him for his return. I hate myself for needing him.

"Come with me," he says. "It is time."

He reaches through the opening in the curtains and takes my hand. I follow him. At the end of the hallway he opens a door I hadn't seen before. This strikes me as odd. Did I merely overlook it, thinking it was, perhaps, a closet? Or had it been concealed somehow? Behind it is a flight of stairs. We climb upwards to another door which he opens onto the roof of the house and a widow's walk.

"It is time to look at everything. It is time to gaze at the vanishing point."

COMMON PLACE

BIRDIE

OCTOBER NEARED ITS END and the harvest was in. Birdie and Bud relaxed at the kitchen table, morning chores finished, mild little Annabelle in her playpen babbling to her ragdoll, the other children off to school on the bus. They'd moved them this year from Common Place to Greenleaf Elementary. It was best, Bud said. Even though they were farther from home, it would be better for them to have more choices, not just in what they might learn in the classroom, but in the choice of friends—youngsters with a diversity of backgrounds, different religions, things like that. Common Place had become maybe just a bit too insular. He said "insular" like it was a new word for him, like he'd heard it at the barber shop downtown from those who considered Common Place a bit cultish. Birdie wanted to ask him what he thought the harm could be. Didn't the two of them attend the country school, and what harm had it done? But right away she knew what he'd say. He'd look at her with that one dark eyebrow of his raised and say, "Just look what happened to Will and Bee." As though the loss of both of them could be traced back directly to the Common Place school and the church that supported it. Bud had stopped going to church. He missed seeing Will there, she was sure, though he hadn't mentioned it to her—not once.

She asked him anyway. What he said was just a fraction off the mark of her prediction. "I'm sick of all the preaching about the devil and his hell. I just don't believe that shit—excuse me, Birdie, but I don't. We both of us knew Will and Bee better than probably even their parents, and we were close, weren't we? I mean, you could say, you could *use* the word love. It was more than just a liking. I would have done anything for Will. You know that, Birdie. I would have fought and died for him had it come to that. But what he did there at the end...the pastor's devil would have danced around his bonfire welcoming Will to hell for that kind of thing. You know it. I know it. But I can't condemn him. I won't. Walking in Will's shoes I might have gone the same way. And I can't step one foot inside that church again and at the same time be loyal to my friend." He sat for a minute, staring out the kitchen window at the cut fields. "And you know what else? God himself wouldn't go inside such a church. Jesus would have been ashamed to go in there."

And that was the end of it. Bud took one last gulp of his coffee and set the mug down hard on the table. "I'll be in the barn," he mumbled as he pushed his chair back on the linoleum floor and let the screen door slam as he left the house. The noise startled Annabelle who began to cry so that Birdie went to lift her up, cuddle her, murmur, "It's okay, Annie," and hum a little until she quieted.

It truly had to be okay though. People have their ways. They have their thoughts. Ways get stuck in your mind, and after that what can you do? This was what Birdie was thinking after Bud slammed out the door. Will and Bee—they had their ways and their thoughts and now were gone. Thoughts are winds that blow people apart. Also there was that fact. Just a fact. What could anyone do about it? Bee was gone, and maybe she never would come back. She'd gotten lost somewhere in this great wide world. But all Birdie had to do was let her mind go loose to be with her again, remembering.

After Bee read *The Divine Comedy* she wanted people to call her Beatricé with the Italian pronunciation and the accent over the final e. Of course no one would. Birdie tried, but it wasn't just their classmates who snickered. Such affectations couldn't be permitted in Greenleaf High or anywhere in the whole area, Common Place obviously included. There were ways of discouraging such behavior. Birdie tired of the snickers faster than Bee did. She never did stop introducing herself as "Beatricé" so far as Birdie could remember now. "Bee's a nickname," she argued. "I prefer my real name." But given names sounded pretentious somehow in their part of the world. Men and women, both, cut their names short, or more accurately had them cut short right from infancy, and so they went through life as Bee and Will and Bud and Birdie. There were even people who seemed to have lost their name altogether, having it replaced with something like a metaphor of their personality. There was Windy Larsen, for example, or Tuffy Jones. Birdie herself wouldn't have been Birdie if she hadn't started to chirp and sing while still in her cradle. Her real name, Bernice, was used at her baptism, her wedding, and probably wouldn't be spoken again until her funeral. It's just the way it was. The only person Birdie knew whose real name seemed normal was Miss Mathilde. And the longer she was the teacher in Common Place, the more normal it became. Though Birdie herself had heard a few older people who had never been her students call her Tilly, a name that didn't fit her dignity at all.

Maybe Bee's common name didn't fit her either. Maybe it was too small and she felt suffocated by it. Beatricé might be the most spacious, most beautiful, most holy, happy name there could ever be. Maybe Bee had needed that wideness of being. Birdie remembered the quotation from Dante's *Purgatorio,* Bee had loved, the one she thought defined for her a kind of vocation she seemed unable to fulfill. Were the angels begging her to take this vocation on, as once they had pleaded with Dante's Beatricé? "'Turn, Beatricé, o turn your holy eyes upon your faithful one, ... who, that he might see you, has come so far.'"

What if all Bee wanted was to be known? And what if that could never happen here in Common Place?

Annabelle had fallen asleep. Actually Birdie, while thinking about Bee, had been crooning the old German lullaby, Mozart's *Wiegenlied.* "Birds are asleep in their nests,/Lambkins and bees are at rest..." And no wonder her mind had hit upon that particular melody; both she and Bee were mentioned in the verse. My, but her friend was insistent in her mind. She rose from her chair and laid Annabelle back in her cradle.

It had been the four of them, all those years. It had been like a song with each of them singing a different part. All the tones fit—harmony. What changed? The fault couldn't lie only with the rules and expectations of Common Place, the church, the school. All of that felt right and safe when they were growing up. It seemed the obvious way to get along, and everyone did get along, not just the four of them. Even the ways they broke the rules didn't break the world wide open as it seemed now to have broken—now that Will had died and Bee was gone. But maybe the ruptures had begun way before Will even became sick. Little things you hardly noticed as life became busier.

It used to be that the four of them did everything together. Birdie thought of all the Sundays they stood outside the church after services laughing and planning things to do during the week. Was there a good movie showing in Greenleaf? Because if there was they sure didn't want to miss it, and afterwards couldn't stop discussing it. What, they wondered would have been the pastor's take on that one? Had Miss Mathilde seen it? What would she have done with it in the classroom? Too bad she wasn't still teaching. That was maybe the last thing they actually did together. And come to think of it, before Will died they hadn't seen a movie for at least a year.

Maybe it's just that life happens to you. Normal things cause dissonance and you have to accept that. She and Bud were parents; Will and Bee were not. Then Will became ill. All of them were still so young, just beginning really, in their thirties. You have to wonder what God was thinking. And Bud was right in saying that the pastor didn't seem to know, despite the way he stood in front of them every Sunday holding his Bible and pointing out the

173

meaning of every single word. He didn't know more than Granny Jarvis sitting and knitting in the back pew. In fact she might have known more.

It was the darnedest thing! Bee wanted to be Beatricé and no one would let her. So she either fought them or she walked away. Another person has a lot of control over you if their ideas make that much difference. When Will died the way he did and the pastor wouldn't perform a service for him, maybe that was the last straw for Bee and Bud both. Maybe she was done fighting. Maybe she just walked away from all of them. Maybe she didn't want a bit of Common Place left in her life after that. Maybe she just opened the door of her house, licked her finger and stuck it in the air to feel which way the wind was blowing, and off she went into who knows where. And if that's what she did, well then, she's no better than the pastor ever was—just as insistent, just as controlling, just as rigid and disregarding of what other people think and feel.

Birdie felt tears coming on. That last bit about Bee wasn't like the Bee she knew at all. She might never understand any of it except that Bee was gone and she was afraid. What if she never did come back? Birdie didn't want to open her mind to that, because if that were to happen, then anything could. Anything or anyone could be taken from her. There would be nothing.

What would it have mattered if they all had just let go a little bit. Maybe she ought to have braved the snickers of laughter and called her Beatricé all those years. If Birdie hadn't feared what other people thought of her, then she and Bee together might have been a swath of orange on other people's green. They might have brought some texture and variety to Common Place. And most importantly of all, Bee might have found her spacious place, someplace large enough for her to fit. She might still be in her house by the alfalfa field and the stand of birch. She might have stayed.

KARYN

KARYN ARRANGED BRANCHES of deep red sumac in a Depression glass vase of cobalt blue and set them in the center of the round oak table. Her mother's vase. Actually, her grandmother's, but given to her mother at her wedding. She'd been thinking of her mother quite a lot during these days of pregnancy, as she sequestered herself in the house she had occupied all her life. There were days that she went from room to room, talking aloud to the quivering fragments of her mother's spirit each room held. She told her how she'd had to quit her job altogether and live simply on the bit of inheritance she'd put by. She felt grateful, she repeated in every room, for the money and every other thing, especially for the love which had begun to seem a stronger force than every loss. Her mother once had carried her as she now carried this child made with Will. Had she ever thought to be grateful for that precise thing before? Had she ever considered the depth of love such a commitment to her represented?

As the days went on, life seemed to slow down. She breathed deeper, moved from place to place around the dilapidated farm with a kind of resignation. She'd lost her fear of people discovering her condition, though in the rare times she appeared in public no one seemed to notice her. At first her invisibility troubled her. How could they not notice? Every third week she went to town for food, and every time people looked past or through her. At first, even though one part of her felt glad that it was so easy to keep her secret, another part of her wondered if people would react if she accidently bumped into them. Maybe she was the dead one and didn't know. Maybe she should test it out. So she did that. She bumped right smack into Miss Mathilde one afternoon coming out of Hartz Grocery, and the teacher apologized. "I'm sorry, Karyn. I should watch where I'm going." So, she wasn't dead. And Miss Mathilde didn't notice her condition; a surprise, since Miss Mathilde had a tendency to notice every little thing.

That was when Karyn started to relax a bit. And that was also when she started talking to her daughter. She named her Zoë after the words inscribed on a cross Miss Mathilde gave her when she graduated from eighth grade at the Common Place school. Miss Mathilde said it was a copy of a very ancient Byzantine design with the Greek words *zoë* and *phos* on the beams.

p

h

z o ë

s

It meant "life" and "light." She still had it, in a wooden box with a velvet lining that Will gave her on her birthday a few years before he died. It didn't feel right to wear it, not sure that she was worthy of it anymore. At the same time there was that saying in the Bible about not keeping your light inside a box. But maybe for safety's sake it would be okay—at least understandable. And life in a box—well, for the time being, at least, she was holding life right inside the container that was her own body. Zoë. The perfect name.

She told Zoë stories about her father, wanting her to know him as the tender and protective man he always was. In the telling she began to smooth out some details so that her memory would match the feelings she wanted Zoë to have. She didn't mention that he hadn't married her in the normal way. She didn't mention how he had died. She didn't mention Bee who disappeared. Of course there was no mention whatsoever of the desperation they both had felt and how the pain of it gushed out into the sex that helped them, if only for the moment, to forget. She didn't mention how it hardened her, chiseled at her insides until it uncovered a vein of rage, of hatred and of guilt. Zoë didn't need to know all that. Mustn't know. God forbid that she should know, and God forbid that such an experience should ever touch that worthy child's life.

Karyn told Zoë about how Will protected her when she was a girl, how he walked her home from school, how he asked to marry her and from that moment onwards they actually were married in the eyes of God and every other way that mattered. They loved each other beyond this world. And she, their Zoë, was the outcome of that love. She was their life.

Was this a lie? How could it be a lie when it was so beautiful? She could feel it changing her, taking fear away, and filling her with something she'd never felt before in all her earthly years. It was the desire and the conviction to protect this life. And that meant both Zoë and herself.

When Zoë was born, maybe as an arrival gift, Karyn could give her the cross and the little box from Will. It would be the right thing to do, because Zoë would be worthy.

MARNIE

WHEN KARYN CAME into the clinic, obviously pregnant, Marnie almost swallowed her tongue. She hadn't seen her since the last Bible study meeting back in the summer, just after Bee disappeared. She hadn't seen her and hadn't questioned it because Karyn was a bit of a recluse anyway. But this was amazing. Definitely pregnant. Marnie guessed almost six months, and she didn't look well nourished. Well—not surprising. She hadn't been to the doctor, at least not here in Greenleaf, and knowing Karyn, she wouldn't be likely to travel anywhere else. What in the world could have happened? Marnie went through a mental list of men. Who would do this to shy Karyn? No one. None of the men she knew. Could she have been raped? Then why wouldn't she have come in? Shame?

"Hi Marnie." She was standing by the desk. Marnie collected her wits. *If you can keep your head...* And right now it seemed she wasn't doing very well with that. But Karyn was acting as if everything was normal. How odd.

"Karyn!! What brings you in?" Stupid—stupid! Not the right thing to say. She ought to have started with something more simply friendly like "what a long time since I've seen you. Has it really been all summer?"

But Karyn laughed. "Just hoping to make an appointment," she said. "For a check-up."

What does one do now? Pretend as though nothing had changed? Mention the obvious? She'd known teenagers who actually didn't know they were pregnant and just thought they'd gained weight. But Karyn wasn't a teen.

Karyn helped. "You can probably see that I need one."

"Oh..." Marnie could feel her face flush. A few single women actually planned pregnancies these days. She ought to have thought of that. Karyn was alone, after all, even more so than Marnie was. Maybe she had planned this, gone to Fargo or maybe Grand Forks for artificial insemination. Maybe she needed companionship and a baby could provide that as well as a husband—maybe better. All these maybes came in a flash and greatly relieved Marnie who didn't allow herself further questions about the theory such as why Karyn wasn't getting her checkups in Fargo. "Of course," she continued her sentence with barely a pause. "When's the baby due? This must be so exciting for you. I've sometimes considered going this route myself." It wasn't true but over the years behind the desk at the clinic Marnie had discovered that most people were comforted and made less tense if they felt she somehow shared their experience.

Karyn seemed to be one of those, on that day at least. "I am—excited. At first I wasn't. At first I was scared. But I'm over that now." Her voice took on a confidential tone. "I've even named her."

"Oh! So you know already that it's a girl?" This was getting easier.

"I'm pretty sure. Intuition or instinct or something."

"Lots of pregnant mothers claim to know even before tests are done."

"Zoë. That's her name."

Marnie smiled. "That's pretty. Is it a family name?"

"Don't you remember? Back when we graduated from eighth grade and Miss Mathilde gave us each a gift? Well, mine was a cross inscribed, *zoë*. She told me it means life."

181

"What a perfect name." Suddenly Marnie felt the whole conversation turn strange, even surreal, and Marnie began to leaf through the pages in her appointment book. "Let's see. Let's find you an appointment time." She ran her index finger down the calendar page. "I've two times on Friday. Eleven and one-thirty. Which is better for you?"

Karyn didn't even hesitate. "One-thirty. It's easier to get into town in the afternoon." And Marnie wrote it down both in the book and on the little appointment card which she put into Karyn's hand.

"See you again then," she said. "You take care."

"Oh I will." She turned towards the door, pushed it open, and then looked back over her shoulder. "Thanks, Marnie, for being so nice. I really appreciate that." And away she went.

For one of the first times in her life Marnie came near to wishing she was an ordinary gossip. She'd known Karyn all her life and never—never would she have predicted such a happening as this. If only there were someone she could share this with, discuss it, try to figure it out. But there wasn't. That would be to *lose her head*, and she had practiced the art of keeping it for such a long time that letting it go just wasn't in her.

MATHILDE

MATHILDE TOOK the afternoon off to visit the cemetery at Common Place. Actually she wasn't taking it off from anything in particular because she was retired now, but even as a retired teacher she had her schedule and felt more busy with important tasks than before. And since the death of Will Fenelon her most tender and grieving focus seemed to be primarily upon him. At first it was just a shocked "why?" But as the weeks and now months went on the question became more of a study.

She had been surprised, she admitted to herself, when he married Beatrice. Intuition told her that the two had little in common. There was no question but that Will would remain in Common Place all his life, while Bee... she ought not to have. Well, she was gone now. Mathilde could barely think the word, gone. She missed her, but not just the fact of her presence in Common Place, but the dream Mathilde had for her, the hope. Gone. She could, she knew, interpret that absence more positively. She could tell herself that Bee had gone to fulfill that hope.

Whereas, Will. Dear, sweet William Fenelon. It wasn't particularly surprising that Miss Mathilde would end up devoting her more motherly energies to him. In general, she had always preferred her boys.

Boys—clear, simple, never holding a grudge. Of course they were bundles of mischief, but that was to be expected. Quiet Will. Kind Will. She supposed that she had loved that boy a bit too much, but never showed it. She wasn't one to play favorites. She might *have* favorites, but that was where it ended. They would not get special treatment from her no matter how sweetly her heart became involved. That was her position up until a month or so ago when she remembered those years of visits from Bee. Somehow, as that was happening she hadn't considered it special treatment.

She cried, actually sobbed, the day they carried Will's body out from the woods. She locked her door and closed her curtains and didn't see anyone for two full days.

She'd taken the day, now, to visit Will's grave. She had some thinking to do. She stood for several minutes just looking at his name engraved on the granite stone outside the cemetery grounds. It still didn't seem right. It also didn't seem right that Bee hadn't been there when the stone was laid. Will's father had taken care of it—Paul Fenelon, the only family member left. Mathilde and Paul were about the same age. She couldn't even remember not knowing him. He'd looked at her and his face seemed old. "A father shouldn't have to bury his son," he'd said, his voice breaking. It always stunned her, the way people said such obvious things at funerals. She supposed there was nothing else. Death tore off all the loose threads attached to thoughts until nothing was left but what everyone already knew. Paul's hair was white now, and he walked with a cane. "I'm so sorry," she said to him. "We all will miss him terribly."

That was already months ago when nature was newly green. Now the leaves on the weeping birch above Will's headstone were a brilliant yellow. She spread her blanket beside the grave and sat on it, leaning against the granite. A breeze scattered bronze oak leaves and salmon colored maple through the air and across the long grasses towards the cemetery grounds.

Poor Paul. Alone now. Sarah, his wife, Will's mother, died before the boy even started school. How old was he then? Three? Four? She just didn't seem able to adjust to motherhood. She took pills and went to sleep for good. Paul had to be father and mother, and everybody thought he did a good job of it. You play the hand you're dealt, the people around here said, and it always seemed that Paul Fenelon won the game with that little boy. But you never know. Time fiddles away and you never know how the song will end.

Breathing deeply of the autumn air, Mathilde let her mind relax. So many memories of Will through the years, especially those years he was in her school room. Such a good little boy. Sweet William, her secret name for him; she still thought of him that way despite all that had happened. But deep down she knew that something had to have gone wrong— something besides the cancer. The Will she knew would have lived that cancer right through to healing or to life's end. That was how he did everything he set his mind to.

She'd brought her shopping bag along, the hand-woven one, made of natural fibers dyed brilliant colors by women in Central America. Into it she had put Will's grade school mementos, thinking to take them out one by one as the spirit moved her, seeing what they had to tell her. It was over twenty years ago that she'd given the sixth graders an assignment to write about their mothers. It was in May, and she intended it as a surprise gift for the mothers of Common Place. The first graders were making Plaster of Paris hand molds. She hadn't even thought of Will's single parentage when giving the assignment, and she felt shock and shame when she found his paper among those of the five other students in his class. It wasn't an essay but was rather a letter addressed to her. She reached into her basket to retrieve it.

Widow's Walk

The blue lined tablet paper's folds barely held the page together after twenty years of opening and closing, and the penciled in words had faded to a ghost of their original #2 hard black. The smudge of Will's finger survived and on that day brought Mathilde to tears. "Dear Miss Mathilde," she read again, and this time read aloud so that, if possible, Will might from somewhere beyond this grave, hear again the words that had filled Mathilde's life all these years.

I don't have a mother. My dad says I had a mother when I was little, but I don't remember. She went to be with God. Why did she do that? Did she like God better? One time I asked God why she went to live with him. Maybe she didn't like me. If I had a mother I would be very good so she wouldn't want to leave. If you ever want a really good son, maybe you could be my mother. I think my dad would like that too.

Sincerely,
Will Fenelon.

P.S. God didn't answer me. But you always do.

"Oh, Will," she said aloud. "Oh my dear boy," and she began to weep as she always did when reading his words. "Why?"

How could she forget the way he stood by her desk after school the next day, his eyes so clear, his face so readable as she stumbled through her explanation—how sorry, how grateful, how impossible. But it came down to the truth. "I can't be your mother, Will, though I would have loved to be if life were not so complicated. I'm your teacher; you are as good and bright a student as any teacher could want. There's nothing you could possibly do to lose me. Your mother didn't die because you weren't good enough. You are as good as good can be. You are always and forever more than just enough."

She remembered how he began to fidget then, and she realized that she was piling it on too thick. But there by his grave, and just for good measure, she reached to place her hand over his name and said again, "You're more than enough, Sweet William, and I've loved you as much as any mother ever could."

After that anyone passing by the cemetery might have seen her on its edge by the birch trees reaching into her bag and laying one small object after another onto the blanket, and seeming to be talking to some invisible person during that entire time. Sometimes she would laugh, sometimes seem startled, occasionally she would seem to hang her head in an attitude of supplication. Once everything was on display and all had been acknowledged, she sat still, gazing towards the horizon. Then she rose, placed everything back into her bag, folded the blanket, picked up the bag and began walking towards her car. As she opened the trunk to replace the mementos it suddenly occurred to her that for all practical purposes neither Will nor Bee had a mother back then. Two students out of five put in the position of needing to answer an impossible question. What had Bee written? Mathilde had no idea. Maybe she wrote nothing at all, but if that had been the case, any teacher would have noticed the omission. She who had always prided herself on not only her teaching skills, but her sensitivity, her ability to relate from her heart with all her students, now felt quite humbled. Anyone close enough might have been able to hear her murmur

"...the answers were never in me. How could you have thought they were?"

Christin Lore Weber

THE STRANGER'S HOUSE

THE SPIRAL STAIRS

THE DOOR CLOSES behind me. I am standing in a stairwell made of stone such as one would find, perhaps, in a medieval monastery. Its architecture differs completely from that of the rest of the stranger's house as though I have stepped through a door not only into a different place, but also a different time. I stand on a large stone made smooth by what must have been the passage of countless feet. Behind me now the door dissolves, becoming part of the circular well. Amazingly, I am not afraid. I do not feel trapped. And the absence of the stranger does not disturb me. Clearly this is a passage he intends me to make alone. Or else, the passage has nothing more to do with him, but is a moment in my own destiny.

The stairs wind around a center pole made of metal pockmarked with age. Each stair-step is triangular with the point attached to the pole, and all are worn and sloped on the larger side close to the wall. The whole well is no more than six feet across with a steep ascent. I take hold of the pole and begin to climb. As I place my foot on the worn stone I can feel the danger I will meet at every turn. Each stair is as slick as highly polished marble. I feel my first twinge of fear.

Christin Lore Weber

Don't be silly, I tell myself. I'm simply on my way to the widow's walk, just as the stranger has told me. All I need is to climb, and I will emerge on the roof of his house where the view will reach to the horizon— to the vanishing point, just as he said.

I steady myself and place my left foot on the next stair and the next. "At the first turning of the third stair," my mind retrieves the words from somewhere. I look upwards. The spiral seems a cross-cut of a chambered nautilus narrowing as it rises to the center. It is on the third stair I begin to hear the voices.

They are singing in the stone.

I listen. The language is music that I recognize as human and beyond human. I hear no words, but the meanings words hold vibrate all around and in me. I focus and images appear of everything I've known in nature that can make a sound, and as I see each individual thing, I also see its place in the universal spiral. Not just wind and fire, air and earth, with their thunder and whispers, and not just lovers breathing into each other or warriors bellowing, not just the song of whales or the multitudes of birds, but even the dancing molecules, the atoms, the many-dimensional strings of being so far beyond any sense we humans possess.

192

Widow's Walk

I climb. One step follows another and the song refines. I climb the spiral. I am in the well and I am climbing towards the widow's walk.

EMERGENCE

I EMERGE through an opening in the center of a round room on top of the stranger's house. Windows reach from floor to ceiling separated by pillars made of some indistinguishable material that changes as I look. They are wood—white birch, but then are made of steel or silver, then seem to flow like water, then are ice. They are steaks of lightning, then they act as mirrors. But mostly they are fire. They remind me of time's divisions into hours on a clock or directions on a compass. When I look down there is beneath my feet a mosaic of the many gods of earth. They transmogrify in a liquid movement from those I recognize to strange and sometimes terrible images I've never seen before. All of them shine. Even the dark images have an inner glow such as can be seen in obsidian. They settle, and I am standing on the belly of a god, and am made to understand that this is Shiva, and I am feeling his dance of changes as though it is my own.

I look out through the windows at a world I've both seen and never seen. This is a world where imagination and circumstance combine in a cast of light without source; it is the source of itself. In it every color merges yet keeps its clarity. In the light I see all the individual forms of the world as though each contains the spark or seed of the entire universe.

I turn and turn again. I am the dance. The wisdom and fire of the Infinite Formless pours into form, and a fractal of that form is me. As I turn I see in the panorama lives long forgotten and those never until now seen. The oceans and the mountains rise and fall as though innumerable millennia pass in a single glance. I see rainforests turn to deserts and return again. I see the soaring dance of birds, every color, streaming like great currents of air through the skies above. I witness both storms and a stillness completely breathless but totally alive. A multitude of beings rise up everywhere and fall, and I feel myself in each of them, their births and death, their loving and their commerce, their wonder and the compassion out of which each came to be and into which each vanishes.

My vision telescopes, and as I focus in, I see at the first pillar a field I recognize as having been my own. Far in the distance, as though on a breeze through the blue alfalfa, I hear the haunting tones of the stranger's flute.

COMMON PLACE

Christin Lore Weber

BIRDIE

WINTER CAME EARLY. October hadn't yet finished tossing all the leaves from the stand of birch, that brilliant yellow that turned the sky periwinkle blue. She shivered as she walked past Bee's old house. It had been a long time since she allowed herself to sing as she made her way home. It had become difficult even to look now at the way the long grasses had turned colorless, the way they bent, how the deer had flattened some of them to the soil. She knew the paint on the siding had begun to peel. No one cared for it now, and it could not be sold. It belonged to Bee who hadn't yet returned.

The children would need to wear snow suits under their costumes on Halloween she thought as she watched the snow fall past her kitchen window. She'd need to get her sewing machine down from under the eaves where it was stored. She always made the costumes from old sheets—a ghost, a fairy—and painted them with rainbows, stars, and northern lights. She wasn't one for blood and gore. She couldn't bring herself to celebrate, even on Halloween, anything that terrified. She celebrated, and taught her children to celebrate, the thin places between worlds. In fact, this year, she hoped she might see Will behind some gauzy curtain, shimmering. He would laugh and

196

maybe even dance. Bee might even dance with him. Birdie secretly had come to believe that Bee had not been abducted, nor run off to live someplace else, nor been raptured. She would have let Birdie know. Somehow she would have reached through that veil if only for a moment, if only with the softest touch. No. Bee must have died. Her body was somewhere on or underneath the earth. And if there ever had been any possibility at all that the dead could reach through the veil between the worlds, it would be Halloween. Even in a dream Birdie would welcome such a visitation. And more than that, she would believe it.

Better get to sewing. Once the old sheets tore there was no saving them. Usually it was Bud who put his toenail through, ripping the cotton where it had turned ripe. The first time it happened she'd tried patching it, but just like the Bible said, (at least she thought it was the Bible) you can't patch old wineskins. The new material just rips away from the old and you're left with an even bigger hole. She kept old sheets in a wicker laundry basket on the top shelf across from the washing machine. She climbed up on the three-step ladder to retrieve them and then began to collect onto her kitchen table the other things she'd need. She wished she had a sewing room where all the necessary items would be kept together. It made her feel like not taking on a project like this, or even the job of mending. She'd prefer being able to leave things right where she was working on them so she could pick up where she left off after being called away or when she suddenly realized it was time to start fixing dinner. The house was just too small and her family was expanding. Three children already, all needing Halloween costumes, even the baby who'd become a toddler way before Birdie felt ready to admit how quickly time can pass.

On Halloween, just past twilight, she and Bud drove the children from house to house, something you had to do if you lived in the country. They visited the homes in Common Place, but they also went into town where her two oldest children had friends from Greenleaf Elementary. On the way home Birdie glanced towards Bee's house as they drove past, but saw only the darkness.

All day long she'd thought of Bee and of the thin veil between worlds. Sometimes she had pretended she could see ghosts, or that she had psychic powers and could tell what others were thinking or predict what their futures might be. There were times she thought she wasn't pretending, but that those sorts of powers exist, at least in some people, and that she was one of them. You can't hold onto such a thought very long before it scares you, though, and she'd always before just laughed at herself for such childishness. Besides that, the Bible condemned such things. She wasn't sure exactly where they were condemned, but condemnation was a certainty, a result of tampering with things a human being had no business wondering about. So she restricted herself. Mere play, she thought whenever she so much as dabbled and even then she wouldn't think of messing around with arcane aids such as Tarot cards or Ouija boards. Halloween, though, that was okay. Christians had blessed all the evil out of it centuries ago. Now it was acceptable even to remember family members who had died and were awaiting the final resurrection on the Last Day. Birdie always remembered her Granny Goosey whose real name was Margaret but none of the family called her that. None of their friends either. Granny had been like a Mother Goose rhyme come true, and most of those she knew by heart. She told them with magnificent flare and could make up new ones on the spot.

Birdie, Birdie, don't you cry,
Even when the days turn gray,
Just sing your troubles to the sky
And lightly fly away.

This Halloween, after Bud and the children were in bed and sleeping, Birdie stood in her darkened house looking out the window at falling snow. "Do you remember Bee, Granny? I'm sure you must. I think she flew away. Please, if you can, find her and bring her back to me." Nothing is more quiet than falling snow.

Birdie checked on each of her children and then slipped under the covers next to Bud and snuggled close into his warmth.

She woke from deep sleep. Her first thought was death. Something heavy pressed down on her making it hard to breathe. She fought her way up from it. So dark. Then she realized that her eyes still were closed. Open your eyes, Birdie! How to do that escaped her. Maybe she wasn't awake. OPEN YOUR EYES! And she did. The room seemed darker than it ought to have been even without a moon. She remembered the snow that lightens the night even only by reflecting the stars. Then in the darkness something happened that she couldn't describe but would never be able to deny. Bee was there as though she were the very form of night, and she was dancing like a flame upon the snow

Widow's Walk

KARYN

SHE SPENT THOSE FINAL DAYS walking in circles around the house and up and down her road, living inside her body with the child, talking to the child, bearing witness to the miracle. Did she think of Will? She thought, if she thought, of spirals in slow whirls everywhere in her and around her in the way leaves twisted in the wind and a hawk made a slow circle in the sky above Common Place. The baby wanted her to walk. She held her heavy belly with its pre-labor contractions. She'd been warned of these and not to mistake them for the real thing.

She'd become a servant, her body and her mind floating in a kind of jellyfish movement, within/without of what no longer was herself. Or was herself but more simple now. A whirlpool of being in which a new galaxy had formed. She felt everything at once. She was the sky, the ocean, the universe of stars and gases swirling.

Zoë, Zoë, beat her heart. Zoë beat in the contractions of her womb. She laughed. Blessed is her womb to bear such a child. She sucked in her breath and bent, holding her belly more firmly. She could see behind her eyes the darkness on the face of the Deep. She could feel the breath of Spirit. She could hear the Voice over the waters, "Be."

201

Christin Lore Weber

Be again, Will, in another form. And I will be, here, in one who will never be afraid. In Zoë, our oneness of life.

And then her water broke.

She felt a squeeze. It started as a tingle at the top of her belly, and then bore down. It stopped her next to a hay bale that swam in her vision as tears filled her eyes. Pressure built as though something sat on her, a giant thing, a bear. But her whole body felt the grip—a bear hug. Her body that always had been fragile, her body that she'd never trusted to care for itself, that same body suddenly was strong. It was power itself. That power and the pressure it exerted would have broken a lesser being in half. It was the power of motherhood that felt universal, the Mother of mothers. It forced the pressure down and out. She found herself repeating "Down and Out" like a mantra as she breathed through the contractions. Gravity took hold. Gravity would pull that baby out.

Again Karyn noticed the hay bale, oats, she thought. Lots of oats around here, planted with the alfalfa, all harvested months ago. She gasped. Distraction—oats and alfalfa—she'd walked her road as far as Paul Fenelon's field. She almost laughed at life's jokes. Ohhh, bear hug again. She wasn't sure how much longer she could stand. Instinct told her that it wouldn't matter to the baby if she stood or knelt or sat

202

or lay against the hay bale in the field. Zoë would be born.

The push and pull. The more she tensed, the more it hurt, so breathing deep and full into the rush of pain would be the only way to promise herself relief. She laid her body down among the left over stalks of harvest on the slope beside the road.

She thought she'd be in town. She thought Marnie would be beside her in the small Greenleaf hospital, coaching her through this. She had promised Zoë a proper birthing, not a birthing such as hers had been, stuck in the middle of nowhere without help amidst the screams of her mother and the swearing of her father. But here she was, alone, and Zoë would be born. "Down and out," she half chuckled half groaned at the irony.

Right in the middle of the next body-breaking contraction she realized she was wrong. This was the way it was all supposed to be. Someone was standing at her side. Someone was with her after all. Someone would catch the baby and would cut the cord. The sun behind the person caused a shimmering as though she stood in an unearthly light. Miss Mathilde's teachings from the Bible flashed through her mind, *The Holy Presence is a pillar of cloud by day and a pillar of fire by night.* Maybe the person wasn't human but an angel.

Karyn gazed through the shimmering light straight into the person's face. It was Bee, and she was smiling.

MARNIE

"SOMEONE really must have been watching out for you." Marnie straightened Karyn's pillows and adjusted the saline drip beside the bed in the Fargo hospital. "If it weren't for Miss Mathilde's curiosity about all us former students, I doubt that you and Zoë would be alive today." Marnie was staying right at the hospital so she could be helpful to Karyn. And anyway, Marnie found herself liking the enigmatic classmate more all the time.

"I thought she was an angel," Karyn said. "She seemed to be filled with light. It was just before I passed out, I think. At least that's the last thing I remember."

"Maybe you were in some kind of altered state. Who knows? Miss Mathilde seemed to think you'd been lying there unconscious for quite some time even before she arrived, and dear little Zoë, still attached to you. Babies are so resilient."

"It was cold. At first I liked it cold..."

"Your body was working pretty hard."

"I guess it started to snow. It's a wonder Zoë didn't die."

"You had your heavy knit caftan on, remember? Walking round your house and down your road wearing only that. So you must have laid down or fallen when the contractions got too strong, and after the little one was born she just lay there between your legs on the soft knit. And the front of your caftan covered her tender body from the snow. And she was still connected to you, of course. Maybe that was helpful."

"And Miss Mathilde found us."

"Yes."

Marnie smoothed her friend's hair. She wanted so much to comfort her. So far she hadn't spent much time with the baby who remained in NICU, even though she wasn't a preemie. Still the doctors wanted to keep an eye out for infection in an infant attached for such a long time to the umbilical cord. She'd heard it might actually have been helpful for three minutes or so, but once the cord stopped pulsing it became an avenue for bacteria to spread into both mother and child. It wasn't dry, though, so Miss Mathilde had found them in the first hour after birth.

Marnie had received her former teacher's frantic call from Karyn's home phone just after Miss Mathilde saw what seemed Karyn's possibly dead body along the side of the Greenleaf-Common Place road. She parked her car and ran to find the two of them, thank God, alive. But what a shock! And then she had run through the new snow to the house.

"What shall I do? I can't wake Karyn up!" Miss Mathilde's voice trembled over the phone. "Can you send Doc Johnson? Is there an ambulance closer than Fargo?"

"Just stay by their sides," Marnie had said. "I'll take it from here."

And so she had. It was she who banged on the door of the examining room proclaiming "Emergency!" She who called 911 for an ambulance from Fargo. She who told the waiting patients they should reschedule by phone the next day. She who made sure Doc Johnson had his bag. She who locked the clinic door and drove the car because she knew exactly where Karyn's out-of- the-way house was located.

What a scene it was. Miss Mathilde sitting on the hay bale very close to her former student who was still out cold. Underneath her coat she held a baby in her arms, a baby still attached to its mother. She was singing and rocking back and forth. "Lu le lu lay, little tiny child." Her voice sounded thin and trembled. She looked into Marnie's eyes.

"I didn't know if I should hold her or place her on Karyn's breasts. But she wasn't conscious. I thought the baby might fall. But I also thought the contact might wake her up. Wake Karyn, I mean. I just didn't know." She was babbling.

"You did just fine," Doc Johnson comforted as he took the baby from her. "You saved their lives."

Marnie had never seen Miss Mathilde so discombobulated.

The doctor clamped the umbilical cord and handed little Zoë to Marnie. "Take her to the house and find something clean to wrap her in. And hold her close next to your skin to keep her warm. We'll let the pediatric nurses in Fargo take care of the rest." Then he turned to Karyn, placing his stethoscope over her heart.

Mathilde followed Marnie into the house and directly into the bedroom where they found Karyn's preparations for her newborn—the diapers, shirts, blankets, everything necessary. Marnie swaddled the newborn as best she could and as she did so she studied the tiny face. Will. This child looked so much like Will Fenelon. "Look!" she said to Miss Mathilde who shook her head back and forth. They both had the same thought, the same question. Had Bee known? Was that the reason Bee left? And was her knowing about whatever it was between Will and Karyn the reason Will's life had ended the way it did and when?

In the hospital room Marnie picked up the water glass from the swiveling beside table. "You should drink as much as you can," she told her friend. "Soon you'll be able to go to NICU to see Zoë, and I'm sure you are eager. It's so hard when mothers have to wait. And she's so beautiful. I know even a second must seem endless before the doctors say it's okay to move either one of you."

What would it be like, Marnie wondered, for Karyn to see Will alive again in that little face? Just like Jesus, resurrected from the dead.

MATHILDE

Mathilde sat amongst her books unable to stop thinking about Antigone. Her intuition may not have been wrong, just more subtle than she had thought. Even after everything she still felt a connection. Since the day she found Karyn and little Zoë so close to death she felt sure of it even though the precise lines of connection eluded her. Now those lines seemed to be reaching across time and space, across generations, across families. The key, of course, must be Will's obvious daughter, Zoë. Life, reaching all the way back to a beginning before anyone even knew of Common Place or the United States. Life for life. Antigone in the cave of death. Will dead in his own inescapable cave. Beloved Beatrice gone. Beatricé of the celestial spheres. Did anybody think of that? Had anyone in this hidden place on the border of North Dakota and Minnesota ever thought of Dante at all? Did no one ponder what it is we live out while here in this realm of earth? The play we interact is truly a Divine Comedy in which life and death collide and interpenetrate each other in an act of love and war that unendingly creates the worlds.

It had been the strangest thing. Mathilde interrupted her thoughts for the hundredth time or more since the night little Zoë had been born. She'd never understand it, how she happened to be driving past Karyn's house. It just kept haunting her—what to make of it. Her mind had wiggled every which way to make it sensible. All she'd planned to do that evening was to get into her pajamas and robe, pour a glass of crème sherry, and read. In fact she'd already begun. She was thinking how delicious it would be. The forecast was for the first winter snow, and the very idea of being snuggled up in her big chair with, probably, Antigone (since that tragic girl already had come to mind), and to let Anouilh's pure poetry

209

transform the tragedy of it all into something beautiful—well nothing would be more pleasurable. She'd already taken the Harvey's Bristol Crème from the cupboard above the stove and brought out the glass when she'd experienced the strangest sensation. The light of the setting sun through the kitchen window caught the stream of sherry as she poured. That wouldn't have been so extraordinary even though it was beautiful, except that at the same time she was sure she heard a voice. Antigone's words. "I want to live my life." And even that would not have been all that extraordinary since she'd just been thinking about reading the play once again, except that the voice was Beatrice Fenelon's.

She could have dismissed even that as her imagination had it not been for all that came afterwards, and also that Bee had continued, "Karyn needs you." And she had dressed again and gone to Karyn's house just as though she believed every word.

Now Mathilde took out her journal and her fountain pen and opened to the next blank page, dated it, and wrote in her elegant and practiced hand:

Faced with the edges of rationality, the imposition of an order of law that hinders, obscures, and threatens to destroy the freedom of life's evolution, both Antigone and Will broke through those bonds by whatever means each possessed. "I want to live life and live it fully," they both said even at the moment they watched their caves cemented shut. Does each of us take hold of life that way? We risk, even choose, that the future will close in front of us because of what we cannot live without. We step past the boundaries to claim who or what we love in a desperate quest for truth and justice that frees the soul. I simply cannot know. When I heard Bee's voice and later looked into Zoë's eyes I reached the end of knowing. Jesus, certainly he must have known, rising from his borrowed cave crying out "I AM." Crying, as we all cry standing with nothing at the edge of darkness: "Zoë—Life."

Precious life, so profoundly loved, we die for it.

Christin Lore Weber

THE WIDOW'S WALK

THE PILLARS OF FIRE

WHAT I SEE AS I TURN
SEEMS NOT OF MEMORY
BUT OF BEING'S THREADS
WOVEN INTO SPACE AND TIME

WHAT CAN THIS PLACE BE? I turn inside the circular tower, the flaming pillars that delineate not just the world as I know it, but the expanse of space and time, known and not known—not even imagined. I am inside the image of a dancing divinity. I am in an ecstasy of turning. "Look, look, look," cries out a voice from so deep within it seems not a thought nor a voice like any I've ever heard even in dreams. It is an explosion, a blossoming of cells, a weaving of infinite strings, an interpenetration of countless dimensions. "Look."

Between the fiery pillars appear the fields, woods and streams of my Common Place home. The vision telescopes and focuses in on the house with its porch facing the stand of birches on the distant side of the alfalfa field and of my father working in the field. It is my first heartbreak, a shooting star that disappears before you're sure you saw it at all. My mother is not there.

213

Christin Lore Weber

THE MOTHER ROSE

WHAT I KNOW of my mother comes to me in stories
indistinguishable from fairy tales. I call her Mother-
Rose according to the inflections in my father's voice,
and I see her in that form of the roses that grow tall
beside the porch. "You came from her," he tells me as
he weaves the stories of the one both of us lost, and my
mind conjures the most beautiful of roses with an
infant, myself, cradled in blood-red petals. I am
sleeping in the safety of her joy, in the moment of her
radiance, in the essence of her perfect being. All the
other stories come forth from there. And from there,
that place, the mother goes away.

Away. And yet I still see her before I am. The
stories are imprints of waves left upon the sands of my
father's mind. "She was all I ever wanted in my life,"
he tells me, "but she wasn't strong. Life, I think, may
have been a bit too heavy for her." I want to know
where she is, and he is vague. "Someplace I hope you
never need to go."

Much is forgotten as we wander through
childhood. Or, if remembered, is remembered wrongly.
A crystal goblet has a favored place on a glass shelf
inside a rosewood buffet. The cup is broken from the
stem. I stand and watch it. Maybe I think that it will
heal itself. Maybe I wonder why it is displayed here,

why even saved. Maybe I think nothing but simply gaze. I could have been a rose shape-shifted into glass. Will Mother-Rose return to claim it one day? I tell myself to wait. If I want her enough she will be here and never gone. In all his stories he never tells me where she is.

I am told she held me, nursed me, that I felt her breath on the soft skin and fine hair of my head as she bent towards me. If the flame could liquefy the glass I believe that I could see us through its light. What would I then feel? And this is the mistake. Making the experience a memory encloses it in the cave of the past where reality has been snuffed out. All experience is alive eternally in a flaming world where it now exists. Once real, so it remains. To know it is to be it; to seek it, yearning, is to find it where I thought it had been lost.

She holds me in the flame of being. First cry. First emptiness. First embrace. First food.

For how long, I do not know.

I hear a scream. I feel a slash that sears my skin.

And then the emptiness. Then the loss.

I seek her everywhere without knowing what I seek. I watch for her in the ripening fields. I sit on a blanket at the edge of the yard beside a patch of daisies taller than myself. Blue and red dragonflies land in their yellow centers. I reach out. I want them as I want everything. The need in me is greater than life, greater than the world. Nothing has the density to stay. I feel my need falling through my eyes, my tongue, my ears, my skin. I lift my head to the fragrance on the wind and it blows right through me as though I am nothing, present no obstacle. Constant loss sometimes makes me cry, sometimes laugh. My bones are seeds of her. If I could lay them down upon the ground and the rains would come she would sprout from them. This is a truth I will not ever know.

THE FRIEND

I AM eight years old and sitting on the thick horizontal branch of the oak tree behind my father's house. I see myself as someone I barely recognize. A shift of light through leaves, and a new and different history takes form.

I do not remember this event. I watch with more than a child's intensity from where I stand upon the widow's walk looking through the pillars of flame. Immediately a voice rises up within me. "You remember nothing. This is not memory. This is who you are, combined with what you might have been. It

216

is the making of yourself." The child shimmers in the light and I see vague suggestions of others, multitudes of forms, any one of which I could have been, or combinations of the many. "You have such potential, Bee," I hear my father say to me.

As I hear his voice I see another child coming towards the tree. She's singing. Her voice is familiar though her face is not.

"Wren!" I call from the widow's walk. And she lifts her hand to wave. On the branch of the Common Place tree the child that is or is not myself also waves and calls out to her, "Birdie!" Time and space collide.

The friend is a wiry girl with long barley-colored braids, thick as the vines that hang from giant elms I once saw growing along an abandoned railway bed that passed close to the Red River of the North. The comparison is odd because I don't remember living in that place, but I feel myself running there towards those vines and swinging from them, sitting in their loops, laughing.

"Birdie! Birdie!" calls the child that I am from the branch of the gnarled tree. "Come on up!" My voice bubbles with pleasure. I feel the feet of the barley-haired girl finding the crevices and toe holds, and her arms that reach to hold onto twigs. I feel her climb as though I am the tree. And the laughter rises between the two girls and I am the one who laughs. I don't question the strangeness of this conjunction. I don't ask, "Am I dreaming?" Instead I accept that what I see from the mosaic floor in the belly of Shiva's whirling dance is what has been true forever.

I take Birdie's hand and pull her with me up to the horizontal branch. I love her. How can I find the words for it or the way to string the words together? Language as it is known to us fails. Language requires that I say "when," as if love moves, as if there is time in which love happens. It does not happen. It is what we are. It does not grow; it is uncovered, is revealed.

I take Birdie's hand as though I've chosen. Do I choose to breathe?

Her hand in mine.

"It's Will," someone says in me. "It's Will you love. All the rest is shadow."

Then I see him, off in the distance beyond the next pillar, by the stand of birch which shimmers now like sunlight reflecting off the ocean tides. Birdie the Wren is gone. Gone is the oak tree. In this place of a widow's dream, my hand is empty; my hand is reaching out. He comes towards me. He is blue as the ocean beside the stranger's house. He is deep blue as the endless sky. Is it the shadow cast by an overwhelming sun? Is it life-blood running through the veins before it hits the air? Is it not Will at all but the god of love?

THE FLUTE AND THE FACE

IN THE DISTANCE I hear the winding tones of the flute like a path through the air on which he approaches me. The husband. The husband is a fragment of being out of which life unwinds. The husband is a musical tone uniting earth and spirit. The husband is a fractal out of which proceeds the wholeness to be unwound.

I've been dreaming of betrayal, the betrayal of death that left me abandoned in guilt. I could not save him. Two men: the husband and the stranger. I struggle to be loyal, but the stranger puts me in a trance. He is the flute itself. He is the coming of the new world. I burn the evidence of my trance in the fire he himself created. I burn it in a cup that melts. How can I choose one rather than the other? Can both be chosen? Must neither? Can a third be found that reconciles the two?

The flute plays and the husband nears. I thought him dead. I saw him dead. He was a husk left behind. And yet he comes near. I recognize his face. I know his gait. How can he be here?

I turn and turn again. "Hide me!" I cry out to something. In the wind I hear a song beyond time: *I am hidden in the obscurity of Presence*. I turn once more and hear a voice I know. "Beatrice!" it calls. I turn again and cry out, "Will."

219

Christin Lore Weber

WILL

HE CAME HOME that day across the icy stubble of the alfalfa field. He came home. I saw him outside the kitchen window, and it crossed my mind, how strange that he would be in the middle of the winter field, disorienting really, but I kept on peeling the potatoes he'd brought in that morning from the root cellar. He carried them in the wicker basket Mama made so many years before while she still was here, and Daddy still was here, and I was not yet anywhere. I always thought the basket should be reserved for rose petals, but Will had a more practical mind. He'd shake the potatoes inside it and the soil around them fell through the wicker weave onto the ground. He saw it as a strainer and argued that his using it kept my floors clean and relieved me of the initial task of preparation. In summer with the new potatoes; all they'd need was washing. Sometimes just a little water was enough to slough away the skins, they were so tender. The larger ones, though, I still wanted to peel especially since he'd requested soup, the smooth kind with caramelized onion and finished off with cream. He had a long stride and in summer the ripe alfalfa parted for him like the Red Sea did for Moses.

Widow's Walk

I was lighting the stove when I heard the door slam. He stomped his boots to dislodge the snow. He didn't come into the kitchen right away, and it crossed my mind that was also strange, not like him at all. When he finally did come in I was cleaning up the sink and trying to focus my mind on the soup coming to a boil. I'd always been a bit of a dreamer and focus took extra effort or I'd be cleaning up a bigger mess. Potatoes stick like glue. So I didn't really hear, at first, what he said to me. He was sitting by then at the kitchen table, and already my mind was split between the potato soup, the cleaning, and the thought I needed to make his afternoon cup of strong coffee, so it didn't completely register that he'd said, "I'm sick."

"Um-hum," I mumbled, running water into the coffee pot. His words were merely sound without meaning to me yet.

"You know I haven't been feeling so well, Bee, and so I saw the doc today."

I heard the words. Right away I thought but didn't say how strange this also was, that he would go to the doctor at all, but especially that I wouldn't know. Or hadn't heard. I measured out the coffee grounds.

"Bee!" He stood and came over to me by the stove. He took my hand and the grounds spilled back into the coffee tin. "Look at me!"

I looked at him.

"He thinks I might be really sick," he said.

My heart broke again.

On the mosaic floor of the widow's walk I collapse in tears upon the heart of an unknown god. I had not heard Will fully when he spoke to me. I had not heard his heart.

I'd loved Will since childhood though he'd paid but scant attention to me, always paying his primary heed to those he must have thought more needy or deserving. Already in first grade I watched him from the playground swing as he took timid Karyn's hand and walked her home. I watched with a kind of hunger unconfined to my belly, aching also in my mind and throat and chest, to be the one whose hand he held. Should I be needy in order to be chosen? I kicked at the playground sand, moving the swing back and forth. I had as much claim to neediness as Karyn, and I knew it, but I disdained it in her and decided that I never would lower myself that far. And somehow, even then, I knew that my disdain also made me undeserving. Sometimes I kicked at the sand, launching the swing high, and then pumped myself higher until the ropes buckled and the seat lurched. I watch myself now through the pillars of the widow's walk. Was I angry? Ashamed? Jealous? Afraid? Probably. Children don't question things like that, but just experience them. Some children have parents who will say to them, "I can see that you are angry over this..." or "You seem jealous of Karyn, and she does have a kind of advantage over you in this, but you have your own advantages—your own gifts. Try to think about those and develop them instead of crying over things you'll never have." And that's how children learn what their feelings mean. My father didn't know how to make such things clear to me. And my mother wasn't there. I kicked myself higher, lurched again, and told myself I could do it on my own, whatever it might be. I didn't need a mother, or Will, or anyone.

All of which turned out not to be completely true.

But that was childhood, and for children those events are normal. At least to think them normal is a way of survival. I watched that beautiful boy go off every day, hand-in-hand with Karyn, and it wasn't long before Birdie and I were watching the two of them together, pumping ourselves high on the school yard swings, singing at the top of our lungs. They would hear us, I imagined, and wish they didn't need to go home so soon, and instead could linger, joining in our play. They never did. And it wasn't long before we tired of the swings ourselves and ran off to Birdie's house or mine to climb trees or taunt the frogs down by the creek. Girls are better, anyway, we assured each other. We caught the biggest frogs, named them, put them in a box and carried them home to dress in doll clothes.

October winds ripped the branches bare and once the snow fell early in November parents showed up at the close of the school day to drive us home, especially those of us who lived more than a mile from the little school.

I see the snow from the widow's walk. It swirls around Karyn as she trudges through the drifts alongside the road. Where is Will, I wonder.

Will and his father sat together every Sunday in the Common Place church. By the time Birdie and I were twelve we already sang in the choir, coming early and sitting behind the pulpit, next to the piano. I'd watch Will and his dad come up the aisle and slide into the pew second to the front. We'd sing old favorites to engage peoples' minds with God-thoughts before the service—hymns like "I'll Fly Away," and "The Old Rugged Cross." I knew all of them by heart, so I could keep my eyes on the Fenelon's and especially on Will.

He never looked up at me. Sometimes he'd turn his head to grin at other boys, friends of his.

Everybody knew everybody else, so we all learned early to be careful. "Don't wear your heart on your sleeve," my father would advise. We all learned the art of secrecy early on. "People talk," my father said. "Don't give them anything to talk about." It was a sort of game; what could you say without giving yourself away? What could you say about others without having your words deflect back on you? How could you tread the fine edge between fact and where it tipped into exaggeration or downright lies?

At twelve years old I was just beginning to realize that everyone had secrets. What you saw out in the open was rarely the way things actually were. The most obvious of circumstances could be the most untrue. Anyone's actions might be camouflage for something secret you were not to know. Will, for example, might have been walking Karyn home for all those years to hide his true affection for some other girl.

Karyn and her parents didn't belong to the Common Place church, and were the only family within the boundaries of that community who didn't. Whatever kept them from joining the church continued to be a favorite speculation of the rest of the community. Even the Fenelon's had joined despite the fact that Will's mother once had been Catholic and even after she died they could have driven to the Catholic Church in Greenleaf if Will's dad had been the loyal one. Behind their hands most of the other members snickered that maybe Sarah Fenelon hadn't been strong enough to live with guilt like Catholic rules produced. Everyone at the Bible Churches thought that Catholics were really pagan at the core. Lucky for young Will to have escaped that fate. Shame about Karyn, though, always on the outside of most everything.

Between the pillars now the light shifts. The winter moon upon the snow and the tall white and black of leafless birch beacons me, guides me bodiless out past the tower onto footprints left upon the snow by someone or something I may once have been. Here in summer the meadowlark sang. Here she dragged her wing through grasses bordering the alfalfa field to distract the predator. Here the agony played out of choosing against all odds to survive. Here now is silence. Here Will still walks.

I see him. I do. A shadow moves through the trees, another's, not my own. "On winter nights," I hear him whisper, his breath wet against my ear, "I sometimes leave you sleeping so I can walk through the birches. The moonlight is the closest I will ever come to the living presence of God."

"Will?" I whisper back to him. "Will?"

Who walks through winter and no one hears the cold crunch of sound beneath his feet? Who steps without his shoes onto the glistening sharpness of the snow?

He turns to me, his face a blue veil of light.

On that day he walked across the alfalfa field while I put the potatoes on to boil, the day he took my hands and told me he might be very sick and then led me from the stove to our two oak chairs by the kitchen table, his voice sounded thick. Did cotton fill his mouth? Were we under water? "What?" I asked. The air felt close, suffused with something not breathable. The world got small. Nothing existed outside the house, and as we sat there even those walls began to fade and a thick fog obscured all but the space that held our gaze.

"The doctor said I'm sick," he repeated.

I felt only disappearance. Nothing else. Was my heart still beating? Existence lifted from me. Denial. The word came out of the emptiness. This is what they mean by denial. I had no idea. Who would believe it felt like this? Then, before I had a chance to respond to that realization, the absurdity of our situation (because I suddenly knew without doubt that he was dying, right there, in front of me) began to bubble up from somewhere deeper than my heart. I wanted to laugh. I absolutely must not laugh. I who was nothing only a fraction of a moment before, suddenly was an uncontrollable fountain of laughter, an endless stream of words. And Will whose face was somber seemed an eternity away from me, a paper cutout man, someone I didn't even know. Please, please, please, God, do not let me laugh.

"Sick? What kind of sick?" I started to say when I heard that unmistakable sound of water boiling over onto the hot stove, the hiss and pop and the kettle cover clanging. "Oh, no!" I yelled as I shoved the chair away from the table so hard that it tipped backwards onto the linoleum. I left it there and ran towards the stove. "Damn, damn, damn," I heard myself cry out. "Just look at this mess! Damn it all to hell!"

And as I grabbed a dishrag off the counter to wipe it up, crying as I went, I heard Will leave the room.

I cannot say with certainty I loved him. Can I say it now? What is love once it is affected by time, once the moment we call love has drifted? I won't say "passed." Some moments alter the form of what we are right through to bone. Gestures, words, the sound my heart makes, and when I lie down, the rivers of my blood that when I concentrate I can feel rushing back and forth through all the little tributaries, can, in an eye's glance turn into the strange. No form is permanent.

Time shifted on a hawk's wing in the autumn of my childhood, the season of blood. My father came home in the early dark of late afternoon, his canvas hunting bag filled with partridge and grouse from the burnt gold grasses that bent and twisted into nests among the oaks and maple that grew along the paths leading downriver towards the lake. Sometimes he walked all the way to the lake itself, early, before dawn, to shoot the mallards. News would go out among the men of Common Place that the flocks had been spotted and would cover the river's mouth where it opened into the big water. He'd leave during the night, and I'd hear the guns as first light sighed through the mist that drifted just above the water.

I felt myself as one of them, lifting from the surface, a winged secret. What might be the difference in quality of pain—that which spills blood from a sudden splitting wound, and that other pain like mine. Slow pain through a wound already there, stretching the body gradually to open it in a relentless ache as the

229

blood drains, useless, acrid. Vulva. Vulnerable. Hide
it! Instinct more than anything required me to keep
my own splitting open, my own blood-letting secret.
I'd not been warned. Who would warn me? Did my
mother once feel this way? In Common Place we didn't
speak openly about such things. I watched the birds
fall. I sat with my father in the barn. We plucked the
feathers that stuck to our fingers with bloody glue.
Alone in my room at night, once the birds were gutted
and left to soak in salt water to get some of the wild
out of them, I tended to myself. I changed the Kotex
pad heavy with blood of my own, wrapped it into a
wad, put it into a white pail and covered it tight. I
thought of the bruised entry wounds in the plucked
birds and how I put my finger into the bloody hole to
extract the metal pellet. The opening between my legs
pulsed and strained as though something had stuck
there, and it was the thing causing the pain I felt. If I
could just extract that thing, reach my fingers into my
own bloody wound, would the pain then go away? But
such an act felt wrong, like breaking a secret. So I
fastened another Kotex to catch my blood, and went
to bed where I curled my body around a pillow pressed
against my belly. "Don't let me cry," I pleaded with
the pillow as if I were cuddling against the yielding
firmness of a mother's body, and finally fell asleep.

Widow's Walk

I see Will again now through the pillars of fire
and light. He's up to bat on the Greenleaf baseball
diamond. We were playing Fargo, a school so much
bigger than ours it was laughable. Obviously they'd
have better players with so many more boys to choose
from. Birdie and I were in the stands, watching, even
though I actually didn't understand the game more
than just the basics of hit the ball and run to the base
before getting tagged. Birdie had the better grasp of
what was going on. I followed her lead, yelling the
words she yelled, standing when she stood, lifting my
arms, waving.

Now my heart speeds towards that girl, Bee,
with pity. But I don't want to pity her, not really; I
want her to be capable, to know what she's doing. I
want her to have had the time to learn these things
that all the others her age seem somehow to have
known for years. I wish that I could call to her from
the widow's walk and tell her it's okay. Just watch
and learn. Don't pretend to know what you still don't
know. Nobody knows things to begin with. They
learn. I realize that I'd never understood that about
myself in the Before. I never could admit I might be
lacking something, anything, especially knowledge. I
call out to her from between the pillars. "It's okay.
You're learning already!" But of course she couldn't
hear me then. How could she?

At the end of the row of bleachers, Karyn sat alone. We could have joined her, Birdie and I. All it would have taken was to slip down through the open rungs to the ground beneath and, crouching, make our way to the edge before popping out to say "Hi." Did we even consider it? She always was alone except in the afternoons while we still were in school at Common Place when Will took her hand and walked her home.

It would have been a wonder to have liked her. Yes. I would have liked to braid her Swedish hair, her long hair, that heavy hair the color of cream skimmed off the top of milk just brought into the house still warm. I would have opened my heart to her voice which we rarely heard anywhere, she was so silent. Will heard her. At least I imagined that he did almost every childhood day that she reached out and took his hand. It would have been a wonder to have heard what she might have said to him. What he had said to her.

Was she with him when he died? I always wondered that.

On the night after Will first had seen the doctor, I woke to the haunting, strange but unmistakable sounds of weeping. "Will?" I said low in case by some mystery of mind or time it wasn't Will at all. "Will?" I rolled over and placed the flat of my

232

hand on his back. He was lying turned away from me, on the very edge of the bed. It seemed that his head was barely on the bed at all, and that he faced downward into the unfathomable dark.

"Oh Will, what's wrong? What happened?"

"It's too late now," he gasped. "It's all wrong."

What could he mean? My mind reviewed the past few days. He'd gone into Greenleaf to have the doctor check out that headache of his. Probably just the flu, he'd said before he left, and after he came home something distracted me. He did tell me he was sick; I did remember that. He'd been away a long time, though, so I must have figured it wasn't that big a concern and he'd taken the opportunity to stop by the hardware store. But in the winter dark of night, my hand against the warm skin of his back, feeling the gasps of his weeping, feeling him tense up against my touch as though my discovery of him in such a state were an embarrassment or even something forbidden, a coldness seeped into my heart. An icy terror. Too late. What did he mean, too late?

"Too late?" My voice trembled.

"Why is life so hard before we're ready?" He took a deep, rasping breath. Then, seeming not to want an answer from me to his question, he pushed himself up into a sitting position and swung his feet over the side of the bed. "I'm sorry," he said. "I need to go to the bathroom."

Outside the bedroom window the moon was just past full and its gleam on snow gave plenty of light for me to watch his ghostly white body hurry away through the door which he closed behind him. Something had to be terribly wrong. Most men don't cry, at least not often. But Will absolutely never did. In all the years of our lives I'd never once seen him cry, not even when he was a little boy, not for joy at our wedding, not for grief when we lost the babies. There was no sense asking him why. He probably wouldn't have known why. He lived; he didn't question it. I was pretty sure he didn't choose not to cry. He didn't keep himself from tears because he wanted to appear strong or capable or masculine. Such thoughts didn't come to him. Maybe they never came to him—not in front of me, at least.

He stayed in the bathroom a long time. I watched the moon. When he came back he acted as though I might be sleeping again and said nothing, being careful when he slipped into bed. He soon fell back to sleep while I lay awake watching the moon descend into the west.

Here's what I want to say now: I loved him.
Here's what I must say: I'm not sure I really did.

Widow's Walk

Here are the things I couldn't know:
        Can love find words for itself?
        Does love allow … anything?
        Might love require … everything?

       The stand of birch at the border of the alfalfa field seemed to me a sacred place, and I always thought Will had been drawn to me because of that. His own heart often wandered there, or so he told me on the first day we found ourselves alone deep inside the woods. We'd teased each other that far, past any human sound. The scolding of a red squirrel, that was all, that and a wren's complicated song. I knew of course that he'd been Karyn's boyfriend for years. That's how we spoke of love at thirteen and beginning to acquire for ourselves even things which cannot be possessed. Friends, success in school, awards, reputation for good or bad—it didn't matter which so long as it distinguished you as someone unlike anybody else. Will belonged to Karyn since he first took her hand and walked her home.

       But by the end of eighth grade all of us from Common Place went to school in Greenleaf and rode to and from our homes on the orange school bus. Often Will wasn't even with us in the afternoon because he'd made the junior hockey team that practiced after school. All of winter passed. Often he didn't even sit with Karyn on the morning ride because he got teased by the boys in back whenever he did. So I barely felt guilty on that spring day, chasing him and being chased.

New leaves hung like tiny fluttering hearts from every branch and twig of the birches. Too early in the season for undergrowth, the trees stood in what seemed an endless labyrinthine pattern. The paths, if they could be called paths, intersected six-fold or more. The straight white and black trunks held up the sky. Will and I twisted in and out, laughing, calling back and forth. "Fooled you that time!" "You'll never catch me now!" Flashes of color. Will's blue and gold athletic jacket. My bright purple scarf.

"Look, Will!" I realized I'd never been in the woods so deep before because I'd never seen a birch tree quite like the one in front of me. I'd stopped. It was a cluster, at least ten trunks growing in what resembled a bouquet. I'd seen two or even three, but never this many, and each trunk was thick—it was an old tree. "This must be the mother of the whole woods. I'll bet every single tree in the birches came from this one. I'll bet this is the very center of the woods."

He laughed. "I'll bet you're right!"

Widow's Walk

I can see the two of them through the pillars now, swinging on the branches that lean close to the ground, then climbing to sit together on the largest of the trunks. Was this the true beginning? The place. The time. The scene begins to fade and I am tired. The pillars dim and lose their fire. Outside the chamber the moon is full over the ocean, a long path of light. I sit in the middle of the mosaic of the gods and touch the colored stones that form their features. I am unbearably tired. When did I last sleep? It doesn't occur to me to climb back down the spiral stairs to the bedroom; I lie upon the stones of God. Who is God anyway, I think as I begin to drift off. The many arms of God circle me as I sleep.

The stranger is holding me when I awake to the sound of the green curtains clicking in the ocean breeze. He is humming the melody he often plays on his flute, and I feel his breath stirring my hair. I reach my hand up to touch his face. He continues in his deep voice that vibrates in his chest and is accompanied by the beating of his heart. He is the music. His whole body is an instrument of sound, the very form of music. I want to linger right here in the vivid peace of his body. My own breathing must have changed its rhythm because he seems to know I am awake and slowly runs his hand down my nakedness. Lingering.

Moving. Accompanying the music. I lie still as the pulsing of his heart finds an echo in my every cell.

"Who are you?" I want to ask, but the question seems a sacrilege. I think I know who he is, but the daring required to speak his name could itself be a sacrilege greater yet. So I am silent. I breathe. Then, continuing the music, he gathers me up as though I am water and he an earthen bowl, or I am sand and he an hourglass, or I am blood and he the holy chalice. To be gathered, all the fragments, all the fine slivers of light, all that has been lost along the way, the particles of dust, the tears, the fine hairs fallen, the unfinished thoughts, the forgotten hopes, the memories slipped away—I can breathe again. Who are you? And I know.

THE DOOR

I always saw it afterwards, the door to the widow's walk, and knew that I could open it at will and climb the spiral stairs to the image of gods and the pillars of fire. Something resists the opening of a door. The days that followed I discovered in myself a tenacity of resistance that led me towards pursuits I normally would avoid. How could I rather peel a potato than go through the door? How could I rather scrub the floor of the scroll room? I sought the peace of the ordinary. Or, to be more honest, I sought the escape. I felt more content to be both blind and deaf. I kept my eyes on the blue tiles of the stranger's kitchen, scrubbing them and then polishing them with a soft cloth until they shone, really feeling as though this would be the better work, the more honest use of my time than looking out upon a world that was gone. I loved the stranger's house and the stranger himself. There seemed no reason not to spend the rest of my life here. The past is past. Let it go. And so I avoided the door. The stranger asked no questions and made no demands. Only that one suggestion which he never repeated: The time has come for you to gaze upon the vanishing point. Or did he say to move towards the vanishing point? I can't remember. Best not to dwell on it.

So it came to be that I was on my knees polishing a blue tile on the morning Pia called to me from the steps outside. It was raining on that day so that the world stopped before the ocean began. The rocks were invisible from the vantage point in the scroll room and the gulls seemed to have taken shelter inland. Pia's voice seemed a part of the past. The last time she visited it was to bring and then take Zoë. Such a brief joy the child was. Looking at the tile and hearing Pia's voice I realized that life had begun to seem more past somehow than it seemed present. The only present moments had become those in which I awoke in the stranger's arms, or the moments I spent polishing the blue tile. Did I want to see her? If only I could disappear into the blue tile as I once could into the alfalfa field. She called again. "Beatricé!" I had forgotten that she called me that. Still I didn't move from my knees, and I heard the door open and the sound her outside shoes made as they fell to the floor. "I'm coming in!" she called and I heard the smile in her voice.

I looked up. Pia, always vivid, stood in front of me dripping from the rain. Her clothes, like kerchiefs of every color draped one against the other, resembled a canvas of wet paint, brilliant watercolor laid down and sprayed. Her hair, too, and her face. She was made of water and color. The whole apparition seemed to dissolve and spread across the tile. "Pia!" I emitted a sound between a cry and a laugh. "You're soaked!"

She grinned, and it was then that I noticed that her face was a mass of wrinkles. She'd turned old, just like everything else. How does one account for such a thing? Hadn't we just recently been swimming in the mountain creek? She had been young then. She had been youth itself. Look at her now! A crone. Old Anna from the Bible. Hecate who carries the lantern to the boundaries of the underworld. Anath who brings the end of times. "What happened to you?" I sat back on my heels and stared.

"Get up!" she ordered me in a voice almost like that of a man. Deep as the rumbling earth. "Get up and get to work!"

"I am working," I countered.

"You are NOT. This is not what you came to do, and you haven't much time," she hissed. Hissed? Could this really be Pia the playful, the tender, the gentle, Pia the lovely, Pia the beloved?

"Time for what?" When did I return to being a little brat?

"How can you have received such gifts and not the courage to use them? What do you see here?" She struck a pose. Her long white hair hung in wet ropes past her shoulders down over her breasts. "What you see is what you are becoming as you walk every day past that door and do not open it. Face the terror or wither, become a dry stalk, a broken reed, and die the final death." She pulled me up off my knees. "You get up!"

I did as she ordered and followed her to the door. "Open it," she ordered.

I opened the door.

PERSPECTIVE

AS I STEP onto the spiral stairs I return to the present, and with my emergence onto the widow's walk time converges, and although this also happened on my first visit I was not so keenly aware of it as now. It isn't so much an experience of time as of perspective, or of that to which I am present and is present to me. A sense of this grows from a notion of past/present/future through a vague or confused experience of having no position from which to perceive, to one of a unified awareness of reality.

God once placed in a woman's hand a hazelnut containing in itself both cause and effect, all that IS, and all at once. Therefore nothing is out of place. "All will be well," she realized, "and all manner of things shall be well." How can it be otherwise? I'm thinking this as I climb the spiral stair to the chamber of vision, of seeing everything and nothing and receiving, in drops of rain that fill me to the brim, the consciousness in which they both have always been the same.

I come to the top and step into the chamber onto the mosaic of the gods and into the rhythm of the dance. Now the divine play of creation and destruction is me, the bone of me, the clicking bone I hear in the green curtains of the room in which I sleep. It is the dance. A dark dance now, a triple helix of divine

242

energies. The darkness of time dances with the light of eternity. Illusion and Compassion spiral one another around the Tree of Life. This music is both the depth of silence and the fullness of sound. How do I know this? I don't know how I know. It is what I am.

I hear Pia's voice again challenging me to face the terror. "It's a series of concentric mirrors," she is saying. "Don't you yet see? All of life, the whole universe is an echo chamber of the word of God. Listen. Do you not yet hear?"

WITNESS

WHITE BLINDS ME. White and the bland revisions of white, the sterile varieties of antiseptic. Against the sterility we walk through a maze of halls at the Fargo hospital, Will and I, early in the morning of his surgery. I dissolve into an emptiness. He walks tall, land-man that he is who can walk through or into anything. Time for tears is past. Accepting this surpasses any understanding I possess and I cannot ask him how. They will cut into his brain. Do I love him? Does it matter? The smoldering pillars burn deeply red, and I wonder, if I throw myself between them will I end up again held in Will's arms? This widow's walk is certainly a dream from which I will wake up. Why not also his illness? Why not his death? Why not the stranger's house? Why not even Common Place and everything I ever thought real, stable, firm, not to be questioned? If I knew what I now know might I have taken his arm to hold him back even from his next step?

We walk as bits of color, reflections on the sterile walls. We are like the many-colored scarves of Pia's rain-drenched coverings. We are tatters of our lives, heavy with impossible desires. Don't die! I must love him if my heart and breath are pleading for his life. All I need to do is be aware of what has held me in this place from birth 'til now to cancel doubt. I glance at him. He is beautiful.

I turn a fraction only and fall to my knees. Before me is a scene far from the sterile walls. Here is the living presence of beauty I didn't see, not because it isn't visible but because I'd made myself blind. Here is the vivid beauty of the world of which I had noticed only the coverings, noticed almost as though they do not exist, noticed as backdrops to myself. I walked through them as if they were stage props. But now they shine. Now they are alive, even divine. I catch my breath. How can I not have seen? Not only nature, but its works as well. Not just the birds, but their music. When I saw them fly, how did I not see the miracle? When they sang, how did I not hear the voice of God?

The people are there too. I walked by them. I walked by them! I did not see the splendor. I see multitudes. I see my father. My mother is holding me. How is it that now I know her? I see Birdie and Miss Mathilde. I see Karyn. I see Will. I see Will filled with brilliance that for the first time I know is love for me. How can I not have seen?

My whole self breaks open in a flood of sorrow. Why did I resist so much the flow of love? Did all I touch turn dark, brittle, forsaken, and then die? I lie on my face where Kali, the destroyer of illusions, dances with her swords and her garland of human skulls.

The chamber goes dark.

Will takes my hand. I would know his hand in any darkness, even apparently in death, for he is surely dead. I saw him there, lying under the birch trees along the path. There was no doubt. I touched his hand already cold. And later on we buried him. I walked behind his coffin—the swaying of my body, every step carrying me through fields of shattered glass although I left no trail of blood. How could there not have been blood? They lowered him into a woodland grave in Common Place. If I could have spoken I might have told them he wanted to be put to rest beyond the fields among the birches. But I could not speak. It happened despite me.

I was not innocent in all of this.

But still he takes my hand.

I had sung to him among the birches. It was my final sound until I heard the earth falling on the wooden box that held his body. A deep groan then issued from my throat, and one word—betrayed.

In darkness of the widow's walk now, feeling the stone image of Kali beneath my body, I think of Miss Mathilde and the little Common Place school. Such places still existed when I was growing up which was not so long ago. It is only when she retired that the school was thought too primitive to continue. It was not primitive, however, so long as she was teacher. She taught the classics, as she saw fit, despite what our parents might have said had they become aware. If she was charged with our learning to read, then why not teach us to read the Greeks? The ancient Sanskrit myths? We knew the Bible stories from our little church, but she added context. The Songs of Solomon, she told us, were so similar to canticles in Babylon as to have originated there. And the story of Job was told throughout the Middle East. Who knows who told it first? The storytellers roamed about from India to

China and took detours in between. That's the way it was. Imagine when the story-tellers came to visit the encampment with their bells and robes and voices that could change to mimic any type of person, even Jehovah. They would demonstrate through their own dramatic voices, gestures and the expressions on their faces, the various gods conversing one with the other.

We turned the stories into plays in which the Hindu gods and goddesses met the Greeks, and often Jesus came into the mix with his heart big as the universe to resolve their differences. Miss Mathilde laughed. "It probably doesn't really work like that," she said. "But then, no one really knows." We drew names of the gods from Will's baseball cap, and the name of the god we drew, that was the god we would be for that day. More often than not, I drew the name of Kali.

Who is she? I wanted to know as much as possible about her. In Miss Mathilde's briefcase (in order not to leave them in the school house) she kept pictures of the most famous gods in every culture. She brought out Kali, and I was amazed most by her long red tongue. And after that of her necklace of human skulls, her sword, and fire, and dance on the skeletons of humanity. "But she is also the Divine Mother of us all," Miss Mathilde said. "The Hindu sutras tell us that She is Time, it is the meaning of her name, 'dancing the cosmic dance on the breast of eternity.' She is rapture in the heart of a human being."

I was about ten years old. I looked right into her eyes and announced with all the solemnity and certainty in me: "You are wrong. The rapture in our hearts is Jesus Christ."

I still see her smile. She nodded. "That's right, too," she said.

Is it a wonder that I needed Kali and Mathilde, both, child of no mother as I was? She holds me now, Kali does. She, the dance of Time's darkness and its blood. Warrior goddess. Destroyer of illusion, of evil, of injustice. Is there no truth but that she requires it?

Is it she who insists upon my never truly having loved the husband?

When all I knew of him was Will, perhaps I loved him then. Perhaps I loved him in his illness because all his power was gone. But in the middle of our lives, in the day to day, in his insistence upon his own way, upon his being always right, did I love him then? Did I love him when the baby died and he blamed me? Might Kali then have danced upon his mind? But all I knew of Kali came from Miss Mathilde's stories then, and I hadn't yet experienced firsthand the dark force of Time from which arises all we touch and love. Nor had I yet identified her equally magnetic inhalation which sucks from us everything we crave until our ever-tightening grip on it requires her to sever the bonds we have to earth and to the bodies by which we are here so briefly bound.

When Will made love to me—I can see us now in a tiny glimmer of light cutting through what is otherwise darkness absolute—I called on her. It was instinct. If I cried out her Hindu name, Kali, in my Christian voice, I do not know. But I cried out for a Divine that fit this female form, that was the source of a power beyond my own, a power of creation and destruction more potent than oceans or than the fiery waves of the universe with its galaxies that swirl from their beginning to their end. Who in the pantheon of a Christian heaven might a woman call upon? We were so young. We knew almost nothing of what this "making love" might be. Who would have taught us? We'd never heard that sex might in any way be sacred. We squirmed and fumbled. Of Kali I knew only what Miss Mathilde and instinct taught: dance of time upon the body of eternity. My heart cried out in the language known only to the heart—"Kali! Mother! Kali-Ma!" And she came into me.

"You are the Kali, upon whom you call." I heard a whisper quiet and as explosive as the stars.

"We are the same." And Will's and my first child was conceived into the realm of Time.

"I was afraid I couldn't do it!" Will laughed. "I'll be damned!"

Was he? wonders my Christian soul.

I turn upon the widow's walk. The pillars of fire flame high. I watch below as Will and I prepare for this new being, not only that of the child but the motherhood, the fatherhood each of us would put on like clothes. How often did I wonder if those clothes would fit? Here on the widow's walk, though, I live the underside of each experience, the dimension of feeling I could not tolerate before. There are feelings that in the early years of life will not come to consciousness; they exist on planes too high or deep for knowing. The most ecstatic or most terrible can take place not to be seen into until afterwards, until our later years, and sometimes not at all.

During pregnancy I again borrowed books from Miss Mathilde and read the ancient wisdom that was the foundation of the myths which she'd neither told us as children nor would have expected us to understand if she had tried. Maybe even she didn't understand. Reading, I would stop, staring at the birch stand across the field, and attempt to let the reality of those stories and those gods find its way into my heart. It seemed to me that what my body tried to achieve had first happened to these goddesses and gods. I let go of the notion I'd had as a child that they were people. It started to be clear to me that each of them was a formless universal energy or spirit to which the minds and hearts of mystics in all cultures had given form. What was happening to me and to the child forming in my body happens simultaneously in the cosmic world, the celestial spheres, the Heaven of heavens. I read the *Bhagavad Gita*, I read the *Song of Songs* and the *Lamentations of Jeremiah*, I read Plato. I'd heard the pastor read the *New Testament* stories on Sundays in the little Common Place church, but I read them again and gasped with amazement at the cosmic visions of St. Paul. Someday, I promised myself, I will understand at least a portion of this reality. My body itself confirmed what I read. The whole experience of life is a paradox, I told myself. I took a deep breath. Oh no! I thought. Will I ever be able to protect this life in me now or afterwards? Any illusion that I could, at least according to the wisdom of the ages, would be dissolved by the divine energy of Time itself. Then it was as though all the gods joined voices to assure me: "In terror's dance I exist in all beings as Compassion."

Of course I know what happens next. I lived my life from that point forward caught in the image of what happened next—the image of blood. The child bled out onto my kitchen floor. As I watch I see that the Beatricé who was my essence seemed to feel, in the ways every woman would feel, that hollowing. The harrowing of the inner field. The flood ravishing the ground. My essence at that moment became emptiness. What happened took place in the ordinary world of Common Place. The seen world. The world of Birdie and of Bee. Birdie who appeared in human garments as the compassion of the gods. But she was not enough to heal the harrowing. Will witnessed and neither was he enough. He wept. I cursed him.

I cursed him! I threw his "I'll be damned" back into his face. He had annoyed the gods, I cried, I groaned, I screamed, I wept. Although I knew it could not be true, I didn't take it back. He tried to comfort me. I shook my head. I pushed his hands away. "You betrayed me," I snarled, a wild cat crazy at the edges of the woods. All the while a gentle voice whispered just behind my eyes, a whisper more like light through a clear green gem, "It is no one's fault. It is the way. Betrayal is the curse of human brokenness, the fragmentation resulting from our inability to merge with the gods."

Who could accept such horror? I would need to be an ancient crone who had suffered many nightmares and made peace with darkness to take such disillusion in. I became Job's wife after Satan had his way. "Curse God, curse all the gods, and die!" I snarled through pointed teeth.

Now on the widow's walk tears fall. I kneel and bend my head to the ground. Who could prostrate herself to the inexorable dance of Time? Who could forgive reality its imperfection? Who would be willing to dissolve?

The pillar fires go out. I had spoken without knowing the meaning of the words. I had seen without comprehension of the vision.

I am left kneeling in the absolute dark.

THE SCROLL ROOM

I OPEN MY EYES to daylight and the scroll of the deer. Through the open doors I feel the salt winds and hear surf crashing on the rocks. The hawk circles riding the updraft above the large rock where I sit and once saw the husband and child far off in the mists. "Pia!" I call, but there is no answer. The stranger's flute is placed upon the meditation pillow where he sits to play his haunting melodies, and I hear them in my mind as though they ride the wind, never ceasing, a presence of sound requiring only that I still my breath and listen.

Little by little the rest of the room comes into focus, and I see that new scrolls now hang on the walls along with those of the deer and the mountain. Have they always hung there awaiting my awareness, or is it awareness itself that brings them into being? At first all I see are eyes, open and large, deep, all knowing, magnetic, attracting me into other worlds, not distant but here within the place I stand. These are not only Asian eyes, but also iconic Greek and more ancient yet: the eyes of Africa, India, eyes of the far north, eyes of ocean tribes, of the natives of plains, the eyes of earth. Our eyes.

My heart begins to burn as I accept that I am in a place unlike any I knew in the Before. Acceptance calls to mind an experience I had with Will in the Before. Although he and his father hadn't been part of the Catholic Church since his mother died, one Easter Paul took us to Fargo for a midnight vigil commemorating the moment at which the Christ rose from the dead. Paul explained to us that it had been Sarah's favorite moment of the entire year, and he thought that being there would help him feel connected to her. So we went.

The church was dark when we entered it, but filled with people. We were given candles made of the wax of bees. In my hand the candle felt like a once living bone of something now dead. I ran my fingers up and down the smooth surface. Then in the back of the church the priest intoned, "Christ yesterday and today. The Beginning and the End. Alpha and Omega. His are the times and ages." Paul whispered to me, "He's going to light the new fire from flint now. It represents life coming forth from rock; death split wide open by the Risen Christ." I had very little idea what he was talking about because at that time these were stories and only stories. I turned to face the darkness behind me and at its center, suddenly, a crack of light. It was as though a vast emptiness had been torn open. Then as I watched, the light moved forward through the darkness, dividing into many flames, illumining the faces of people coming through the darkness at the back of the church towards the altar in front. The priest lifted high above him the largest candle I had ever seen. Its flame of new fire flickered, and from it acolytes lit the small candles each of us held. All along the way the priest kept singing, "Light of Christ," and the people responded, "Thanks be to God." By the time the procession reached the sanctuary, the entire church was bright with candlelight.

I was entranced, and even more so when the priest began to sing the song of the Christ Candle as "the wonderful brightness of this holy light...by which the darkness of the whole world is dispersed." He then went on to chant a hymn about the night in which we stood with our flames illuminating the darkness. Over and over he proclaimed "This is the night when..." and as it seemed to me, mentioned all the life giving moments of history, everything the universe has experienced from the beginning, all of it present now, simultaneously as "heaven is wedded to earth and earth to heaven."

Now in the scroll room with icons all around me, eyes deep with visions of eternity, I realized that what I'd experienced during that ritual so many years before was an enactment of an essential reality.

Here, now, in the scroll room of the stranger's house time merges with eternity in the Divine Light of Presence, and as images dissolve into the fullness of reality, I also am dissolving with them.

I look up again at the scrolls and can see iconography from around the world also covering the stranger's walls. And in the midst is a scroll of calligraphy from the *Mahanirvana Tantra*, a prayer to the Eternal Divine One of many forms, recognized as consciousness, reason, sleep, hunger, shadow, energy, thirst, forgiveness, species, bashfulness, peace, faith, loveliness, fortune, vocation, memory, compassion, fulfillment, Mother, Illusion.

Widow's Walk

That power who exists in all beings,
reverence to Her,
reverence to Her,
reverence to Her,
reverence, reverence.

And beside it hung the opening to the Gospel of John.
In the beginning was the Word
And the Word was with God
And the Word was God.

    I kneel before the scrolls until dusk and I hear the sound of the stranger's foot on the threshold. He enters the room. Admittedly I expect him to be dressed in white robes and surrounded by a holy light, but he is wearing Levi's and a red T-shirt inscribed, *NOTHING HERE: GET A NEW LIFE.*

    "Hey," he grins. "Beatricé! How's your time upstairs?"

    "There is no time up there," then I groan. "Sorry," I apologize, "it was hard to resist that one."

    He's laughing. "You're beginning to see, then. Time is not of the Essence. Right?"

    "I'm not sure. Is it like this? There are at least three ways of looking at things—three perspectives, I guess you'd say. There's Common Place, there's your house, and there's the widow's walk. I'm always looking at the same thing, but depending where I'm standing I see it differently."

"Not bad," he says.

"Do I ever get to choose between the three?"

"Is that something you'd want to do?"

"Maybe I could stay right here. . ."

"You don't think you'd tire of it here?"

"True. It's a bit small. Limited. Like a depot, an airport."

"A stopping off..."

"A resting spot, a resort, a retreat house, a motel..."

"A transition?"

"A departure gate?"

"Not yet. Don't you want to see everything first?"

"Must I?"

"No."

"It frightens me."

"I understand."

"I'd have to return to the widow's walk?"

"Yes."

"And I will see?"

"You will."

"Okay, then."

"Okay?"

"I'll go."

But first I sleep. I lie down among the bones that now I barely hear as they touch each other like bees' wax candles in the ocean winds. I lie surrounded by the green. And I dream, but unlike any dream I've ever had because it has the texture of reality I discovered on the widow's walk.

I am a child, maybe three years old. I'm with my mother and father outside our house on the farm in Common Place. My mother! She wears a light green suit. My father also is dressed up—not wearing his work clothes. Are they going to church?

"It's time to go," he says to her.

She stoops down to me. "Be a good girl, Beatricé," she says and tears are running down her face.

I throw my arms around her neck as though to hold her back. "Don't go, Mama!"

"Daddy will take care of you, so well. You'll see. You do what he tells you, okay Beatricé? You be a good girl."

"It's time to go," he says again. "You do what Granny tells you, Bee. You be good until I get back."

Mama lets go of me and Granny, who is standing right behind me now, puts both her arms on my shoulders and pulls me close. I can smell her apron. Honey.

Daddy takes Mama's arm and leads her to the car. She's looking over her shoulder, and now she's sobbing. "No. I don't need to go there...I'll get better." Then the car door slams shut.

Mama is leaning out the window as Daddy drives off. She's crying out, "I love you, Beatricé. I didn't want this. I love you. Remember."

And then the little girl I am is crying out over and over as the car drives away. Granny is holding her back as she strains against those arms—"Mama, Mama, Mama, Mama, Mama..." And the mother is crying back, her voice almost lost in the wind, "Beatricé..."

I woke with words from my depths. "No one told me this. I never knew. I didn't remember. I forgot."

Widow's Walk

THE BIRCHES

THE MOSAIC now gleams white and black. On a field of cold stands a bare branched tree. Gone are the images of Kali and the Christ. Gone is Shiva. Gone are the brilliant stones. Gone, the fire. The pillars that once flamed now resemble stanchions of wrought iron and the widow's walk a kind of pen to hold the wild in.

Winter covers the fields of Common Place, stretching over the land as far as I can see. I know how winter feels underfoot, how the winds have blown the snow into drifts and hardened them, how we walk on water. Thick crusts of white ice. I know the stillness absolute. Sometimes the track of a deer where its hoof has broken through. Sometimes the tiny tracks of the winter bunting. Mostly nothingness. Mostly the sting of minus zero temperatures, frost on eyelashes and brows, air that stuns the lungs and feels like a solid thing, a cold steel sword run through and down into the vital parts.

Amber-colored light shines through the windows from my house where Will and I both sit on separate sides of the room or of the table or of the house itself. He in his woodworking shop, I in the sewing room where I took to making quilts from fragments of the past, precious clothing, my mother's wedding dress, a swath of flannel from a baby blanket

261

never used. I sew in a bit of lace that must have been a fancy collar my great grandma wore. Green silk from my great grandpa's tie. I tried my best to put it all together, stitching not feeling the thin threads of my life.

From my sewing room I hear him saw the wood, the birch and maple, the black walnut. I hear the pounding of the mallet, careful not to wound as I was wounded. Then I hear so deeply behind my mind it must be outside of me. "Or, as I wounded him." No. How could I have wounded him? It was my body doing as a woman's body does. No. It was mistake; it was flaw; it was the breaking of a promise; it was the betrayal of reality. The mallet has a different sound than a hammer made of steel. Softer. Without malice. Almost loving. I cannot tolerate this further. Just when I believe I need to leave, even if it be barefoot across the hard crusts of snow, he stops. I cannot hear the sanding that he does by hand. I cannot feel the way he wipes the wood gently with a flannel cloth and oil.

At night we lay on opposite sides of the bed. To be touched by him would burn my skin, would open with flame the small aperture into my heart, a danger I could not allow. I would not allow myself to sense the flood that would surely happen then, the torrents that would pass over me, the despair.

Widow's Walk

This went on for years. I didn't want to tell you that.

The whole time it went on, I wanted him. Never did I let him know. I didn't dare. How can I say what it was like? There is an antagonism in the soul; how can I tell it? There is a chamber where the longing and reviling meet and grapple. Just to say the words pulls at my heart. But it is true. It is true that we can love and refuse that love in ways that ache and cry and spit and claw here in this world. And we can be sorry and be wild all at once. I chose silence. I chose to turn from him. Did I do wrong? Perhaps I did; we do not always know the right from wrong. Through my life I haven't known always, not even most times, which is which, and I wonder if most people do. Did I love him? This is why I cannot answer that, because I know I hurt him. I know he was as torn as I whenever he thought of the child and of his curse which was not a curse at all but a mere surprise. The surprise of a boy who really didn't know or wasn't sure yet he was a man. And I ask myself, if I knew no curse was meant, then wouldn't God know all the more? And if there were punishment to be had, then who might take the blame? Not God, certainly. Not God. So who else was there? Only Will and his curse, or me. Me and my body which was not good enough. And if not good enough, then why? Either it must be God or me. And not God certainly. So...me. But I know I had no power nor any claim to innocence. Nor even any guilt if it came down to that. But if God? If God, then what remains? If it is God who does these things, these horrific things, these terrible...then all is lost. Lost. And so silence must be kept. Memory must be obliterated. All we believe, in order to be human, must be consigned to oblivion.

I slept on the opposite side of the bed and quieted myself, because what else was there to do? And the years went on.

When Will began to tarry late in town, I already knew. I cooked his supper and laid it out; then I watched the movement of the hands upon the clock. You know nothing, and the nothing I knew came to me in one word, a name, and the name of nothingness was Karyn.

How could he do this thing? I asked the snow underneath the yard light, drifting. "He's done nothing," said the snow.

Where is he then?

"Do you care? Do you turn to him in the darkness? Do you seek his warmth? Do you ask for his forgiveness?"

I did nothing to forgive.

Widow's Walk

"You did nothing."
That's right.
Nothing.

Snow drifted against the house and piled on the roof, deep by several feet. Will said he'd need to go up with a shovel to dig paths for runoff or the rising heat from inside would create pools under the insulating snow that then would find the ceiling's fragile places and leak through. I see him through the stanchions, climbing, catching himself on the icy slick, trying to shovel, heavy, heavy the wet snow, impossible to lift. I watched from the small dormer window as he worked. I wanted to call out, but stopped myself. No leaking ceiling is worth this risk, I thought I might call out to him, but by now I'd become so uncertain of my judgment about anything that I couldn't make a sound. "He knows best what to do," I told myself. But did I believe that? I did not believe that. I believed him foolish. I believed his willingness to stake everything on his deceitful desires. What that had to do with an icy roof, I didn't know and didn't question. I believed that he would hurt me, hurt us, in any of a million ways. And if he fell, then what? He would not be seeing Karyn anymore.

On the steep incline of the roof he laid himself down. With his left hand he held to the side of the dormer. He said later that he knew if a pool had built, it would be where the angles intersect. With his right hand he pulled the shovel again and again, loosening the snow, finding the pool, making a drainage channel, and the pent-up water then began to flow. He held to the dormer and watched it go. Then the whole buildup gave way and the snow slipped like an avalanche under and around him. I yelled, "NO!" But he held on.

When he came back in through the kitchen door he was sopping wet. I was putting the white and red polka-dot tea cloth on the table and brewing coffee.

"That was damned exciting!" He grinned.

"You could have broken something!" I scolded just a bit. "Go in and change your clothes. I've coffee and cookies here for you to warm yourself."

I never asked. Never once did I turn to him, letting my heart speak, allowing my voice to say, "Are you having an affair with Karyn?" One day, early on after the baby died when he first began coming home late, I practiced the words while looking at my face in the bathroom mirror. "Are you having an affair with Karyn?" I lowered my eyes against the reflection there.

Widow's Walk

THE SURGICAL ICU.

WHAT CAN BE SAID:

> White curtains and white walls.
> Muted light.
> Murmur of voices.
> Thump of the oxygen pump.
> A scatter of packaging for needles, bandages,
tubes.
> The way my feet felt on the vinyl floor.

What cannot be said:

> The word for "you were lost among machines."
> The word for the long red gash around your
ear, across your temple, up behind your hairline all
along your head.
> The word for a stripe of hair, shaved.
> The word for dried blood.
> The word for your face swollen past
recognition.
> The word for leaning forward, my head on your
shoulder.
> The word for swallowing my fear.

The word for spooning chips of ice onto your tongue.

The word for leaving the room.

The word for leaving myself behind.

The word for collapsing against Birdie's chest.

The word for tears.

The word that means

> Don't die
> Don't die
> Don't die
> Don't die
> Don't die.

TREE OF LIFE

I LIE PROSTRATE on the white mosaic of the widow's walk. Am I waking from some unconsciousness? The stones cool the heat of me. My heart. "Take from us our hearts of stone and give us hearts of flesh," of blood, of fire, of love. My heart beats against the white stones, and it melts. It has been the heart all along. I thought that it was snow. What does it take then to melt a heart?

I am raised up. There is no sense I've done it on my own, but I am raised above the stones. White. Is this the room where my husband lay? I recognize the feel of it. Now set in onyx among the white I see the bones of a tree. A skeleton. The essence of all trees that ever came to be, whether they be trees of the countryside or the sacred tree of the soul. From far away I hear the clicking of the bones.

I hear from farther still the voice of Miss Mathilde reading to us lines from the dream of St. John :

> *Then he showed me a river of the water of life*
> *On either side of the river was the tree of life,*
> *yielding its fruit every month;*
> *and the leaves of the tree were for the healing of the*
> *nations.*

As I watched each branch of the tree produced a leaf, and every leaf was a jewel, and every jewel was a name, and every name had a meaning. The names were

Ein Soph: Infinity
Keter: Will
Binah: Understanding
Hokhmah: Wisdom
Gevurah: Power
Hesed: Love
Ti'fere: Beauty

Christin Lore Weber

Hod: Splender
Netsah: Eternity
Yesod: Foundation of Covenant
Shekhinah: Presence.

And I heard in vibrations of sound, "It is the Nothingness bound to the Presence. It is the Unspeakable. It is the Never-ending that did never begin. It is the form of the Formless. It is the Tree of Life."

It seemed then that the burning in my heart ignited once again the pillars that burst into golden flame.

"But the wrongness in my heart?" I asked. "The jealousy? The rage? The great possibility that I never learned to love?"

"Become aware," the Voice replied, and directed me out beyond the flames again and into the Before of Common Place.

We drive up to the house—I am driving. It is happening, so it seems, now. The house is older or at least different in a way I'm not sure I noticed on that day as we came home from the hospital and Will couldn't drive, of course, and Will always was the one who drove the car. He lay in the back seat, his legs pulled up, his face bruised, his head still bandaged like

270

a casualty from the First World War. The house looks different, ragged almost, and lit by a kind of radiance I'd not noticed before. I don't know if I noticed it then. I don't think so. If I had I might have remarked, "Will, when I stop the car take a look at the house. It looks different to me, and I want to know if it looks the same to you." But I didn't say such a thing to him, broken as he was, lying, knees drawn almost to his chest, pretending to sleep.

The engine noise brings Birdie to the door. I almost begin to cry. There she is, my friend, ready to do whatever I might need. I want to fall at her feet, embrace her knees. Where did I get that urge, that image? The Bible, I suppose. I seem, here on the widow's walk, to have become a receptacle for the hearts and voices of people of every tribe and nation. My gratitude to her feels beyond my normal capacity to feel. Birdie, Birdie. There she stands and I know there will be vegetable soup fresh from her garden waiting for Will and me, hot, on the kitchen stove. I see her come down from the porch and towards the car. Birdie who is Wren and more. That's what amazes me. In her face I see shadows of women's faces starting with the first of us. It is all one face, Birdie's face, but depending how I look I can see Pia, I can see my mother whose face seemed always to have been hidden from me, I can see all the mothers of history and of myth. I hope my face might be among them.

Birdie kisses me and lays her hand lightly on my cheek. Then the two of us help Will out of the car. He waves us off. He wants to make the trip into the house on his own. We walk beside him anyway, to catch him if he should get dizzy or find himself too weak.

Something's broken in me and a tenderness is flowing through. I didn't break it. I didn't even choose to let myself be opened by whatever power this is to open me. Had it been up to me I would have kept the locks tight. I would not have agreed to the risk of feeling again what I felt when the baby died. And might this not be worse, to lose the husband that I didn't know I loved?

Mostly we lived this time alone. Birdie came and went. Will hoped not to be seen by anyone else until he healed. He refused the pastor, explaining that it had been such a long while since he'd been to church, he just didn't see the need. Birdie came and went and sang to us. Word got around and things got done. Fields, garden, some carpentry on the house. In late April a crew arrived to plow and plant the alfalfa. People are good beyond what I had realized. Food showed up at our door. Little notes in the mailbox:

"Anything you need, just call. I can be at your door in five minutes."

Will got stronger and weaker all at once. I took him twice a week to Fargo for a kind of radiation that it turned out didn't help. It's an odd thing when the brain gives way. He could feel it; I could see it. One night he wanted to make love. I wasn't sure. "Are you sure?" I asked him while I thought of what could happen. Could he have a stroke? Was his body strong enough? "I'm sure," he said so gently it was as though all the years of distance never were. "It might be the last time."

He was unspeakably weak. I moved close to him, not sure what to do, how to be tender enough, how to find that gentle love that must be somewhere deep within me. He was fragile as a fawn born yesterday. He ran his forefinger over my lips, so lightly, with such an aching hope. Was it hope? "I love you, Bee. Remember that. Please remember that." And we both began to weep. I wiped the tears from his face and placed them on my tongue. Oh salt. Salt of the exiled people's tears. Salt of the sea of our becoming.

"I love you, Will. I've been unfair. I kept wanting the baby back, and in that impossibility, I lost you for a time—for years. Can you forgive me?"

He touched the tip of my nose and both of us laughed just a little bittersweet laugh. "No need." His voice was low. "People do what they must in order to survive. You did lose me for a time, but I was the one who went away. Can you forgive me?"

"The moment I forgave myself, I forgave you."

It was true and not true. I wanted to forgive both of us more than was possible for me. Love and forgiveness are only as large as humanity is capable. I wanted both to be infinite.

For such a young man he was not agile when he lay upon my body. Illness had so weakened him. Already his inability to eat made him angular and without muscle, and he lay full weight on me. I hadn't thought he would be heavy. Bones are heavy. I welcomed his weight. I welcomed the breathlessness it caused as he crushed down upon my ribs.

He moved in me. I responded to his rhythm. I marveled that he could have sex at all, but that was later. We danced the ancient dance of life and death. Eros and Thanatos, both lovers in one. "Oh God!" Will groaned when he released.

We lay there for a long time holding hands. "When I die," he said, "don't let yourself be sad for long. I want you to live. I hope you can go away from here, this place of confinement in small ideas. Neither of us were meant for this place. This place took my life."

"It wasn't the place, Will. It was cancer."

He shook his head. "Well, yes. But the underlying cancer is to resist your true life, to hide away your gifts, to make do with what cannot nourish you. If I get to do this over—I mean, if those folks who believe in reincarnation are onto something—I hope we meet again and get another chance to do it right. We got stuck, Bee, we really did. We let death trap us when we could have risen out of it, been free, really lived our lives. We should have a sign, don't you think? In another life after this one I'll wait for you under the old clock without hands in a village square in a town where both of us have gone for a reason that seems crazy but unavoidable. And you'll walk up to me, and I'll say, 'There you are!'"

"Yes. And I'll grin and lift my face for your kiss as I reply, "I've always been with you."

The next day, it was already early June, while I was in Greenleaf picking up some food he thought he might be able to eat, Will took his hunting rifle from the closet and walked slowly through the sea of blue alfalfa to the edge of the stand of birch where he sat under a tree and shot the cancer out through the top of his head.

Christin Lore Weber

It was the hawk. The hawk circled above his
body, lower, higher, lower again. I was driving toward
the house on the way from town and saw the bird at
the wood's edge. It's a deer, I said, but I knew that it
was Will. It's just a deer, the weak one that would not
have made it through the winter anyway. It's nature's
way. Life and death in balance perfectly. But I
stopped the car because I knew but kept my knowing
at mind's length. But for the contrast of the blue of
alfalfa with the birch trees, I would not have seen him
there, propped against the black and white of the tree.
And when I did see him, even then I would not allow
what I saw, that it was Will. The pieces didn't fit. The
splinters of light. The fragments of reality. The blood.
The bone. Nothing made a bit of sense. How could it?
So absurd it was. Where might be that clock? Where
was the town in which he said he'd stand. Where his
words, "There you are!"

I am not there. I'm standing between pillars of
flame on the widow's walk. There is no clock, no Will,
no Beatricé walking there. Does anything exist? The
ocean once surged below. The creek ran down into the
sea. A hawk flew above the pines. Nothing like that
now. Now only the splinters of a life once lived and
lost somewhere commonplace.

In the blue, at the edge of the stand of birch I
stood and gazed forever at what I could never know.

276

Did I do this? I wondered as I stood. Who am I if I did? Who am I now? Who was this shattered man I called husband?

Stillness entered me like ice. I stood beneath the circling hawk beside a thing I could not fix, and could no longer meet, and could not love.

Oh Infinity! Oh Eternal Emptying. I am your bride and you have taken from me everything.

Birdie came. How did she know? She came and took my hand and led me up the path and back into the house. She did everything. She made the calls; she answered the doorbell when it rang; she talked to the sheriff; she stripped the bed and made it fresh; she undressed me and helped me lie down in it; she climbed beneath the sheets and held me; she sang to me when I couldn't sleep.

"He didn't want to die that other way, that slow way. He didn't want to lose his mind, to feel his whole body give way." I knew that, but I didn't want her to say it. Words made it real. I wanted it to be different. I would turn the clock to yesterday. Suddenly I hated Birdie for saying what she did. I wanted to claw at her mouth and her eyes for seeing what I was, what he was, and using words to capture it. I swallowed my hatred like bile.

"Would you want him back like he was? To suffer that?"

I would have. Yes. It seemed to me that our love only had begun the night before. We stood naked to each other then, really for the first time. How could he do this? How could he have thought it better?

How I hated him—loved him. How I raged. How I cried out. How I sobbed until nothing of me was left to sob. How I fell into exhausted darkness. How I slept.

He haunted me. In dreams I heard the telephone and fought my way out of sleep to answer it, then thinking I actually was awake I lifted the receiver to my ear and heard a voice behind a crackling. "Will," I cried out, "I can't hear you. Louder! Louder!" but all sound had splintered, reduced to fragments, bits of things I knew—the chirp of birds, scold of squirrels, the high scream of coyote, surf breaking, howl of wolves, sonar depth charges, multitude of voices in every language combined— scrambled into babble. He was trying to reach me through cosmic litter. The connection was broken. I woke up shaking with sobs.

I didn't know I loved him until too late.

Widow's Walk

Sleeping and waking it was the same. Time and space both fragmented and scrambled. Awake, I begged God to let me sleep, permit me my required oblivion, but asleep I found no oblivion but rather the horror of images I could not bear to witness yet again, of clotted blood on the kitchen floor and of the same where Will's brain had been, and then the same everywhere as though the world of dreams were made not of solid things at all but of all life blown into bits of blood and bone and brain, of feathers and the fine torn webs of worms and spiders and the nets of fishermen. It made only the more fearsome sense. I would wake screaming. Or, awake, I would wander through the house and yard as though my own brain had disintegrated in a blast that took away all thought and its sought-for meaning.

My closest friends visited—Miss Mathilde, Marnie, Birdie, even Karyn—bringing food, sitting with me while I slept. Their voices became unrecognizable as the wind on a winter night. Words ceased to have meaning. Words could have been the sound of wind in cedar boughs, of dry grasses brushing, of rain on the window. A moment arrived finally when I wanted nothing, neither to sleep nor be awake, neither to be alone nor with anyone, not even Will had that been possible. I could not eat the food they brought. Emptiness became a refuge, a place to hide, a way to keep my body from reacting to the world, to life itself. Hunger ceased to exist. My body became quiet. One morning I woke up in the middle of the kitchen floor and I recognized it as the place the dead baby once had lain. My first thought was that the child and I had taken the same path and soon I would find both Will and the child in a different realm. But I'd only fainted. I'd wandered in to fill a glass with water and the next I knew the glass lay beside me, broken, on the floor, the faucet still running and water pooled beside and under me on the linoleum.

Miss Mathilde took me to Will's memorial. From the widow's walk I see it only through a haze. If his spirit was present that day, I didn't feel it, but then I didn't look for him or open my heart to him because the place, outside the churchyard cemetery seemed a wilderness that day, and dangerous without the touch of his hand on mine, without his whispers in my ear. His father was there, and friends. They shared their stories and a few songs. Birdie sang "What a Wonderful World." Will told me once that he figured he would probably end up a pagan, loving the earth as much as he did and disliking the attempt to conform his spirit and beliefs to those of any other man. Miss Mathilde said he was a bit like Thoreau in that respect.

Maybe he would have laughed at the idea of having been excluded from a church funeral and the preacher saying he died too young. Maybe he'd taken up presence down by the birch tree where he sat to die. If I'd had any mind at all during the planning of this farewell, I'd have said he should be buried there, at the place he chose.

"It will get better, dear," Miss Mathilde said and squeezed my arm. "You'll see." But really, I couldn't believe her.

I don't think it did get better.

I can't say whether I am better yet.

MOTHER TREE

Am I still on the widow's walk? The pillars of fire are gone. No mosaic. All barriers have disappeared. Though I seem no longer here, I'm not nowhere. Around me is a sense of something turning, levels upon levels whirling into each other. Faces appear and dissolve into other faces. Human faces that I've known, some whom I've imagined: father, mother, friends that over the years I had forgotten until now, friends I could never forget. Miss Mathilde, Marnie, Karyn, Birdie, Will…Oh Will! Why did I withhold so much from you? All the faces appear as a simple shift of life as it appears, combines, folds and unfolds like a cosmic flower. The form of everything in a single face.

My heart is burning as I watch, and though I do not move, it seems I am leaning into them to be within this flow. I am new to this place and am being initiated. What I saw as trees and flowers now are people, adept at how the elements work. They hold a book and from it can set cosmic forces free. As they turn the pages the color of being and the whole skyscape changes from one indescribable color to another. They are teaching me how to make these changes. Each color of land, air, sky intoxicates. They have me try it on my own. I turn a page and everything changes to pearl rose, a color that is also an elixir. It is ecstasy, as though when the pages turn the transformation is happening in me. All color, all the vibrations of sound, the music of eternal Being from which every form arises and to which everything finally returns—I am not separate from that. Everything both beautiful and broken. Everything belongs.

Then as I watch, the center opens in a silent explosion of nuclear light and cosmic wind that carries me across or through a barrier or rip in being itself, and I find myself unfolding in a different place, a new place. I had looked for answers where there are none, to know what cannot be known, to possess what cannot be had, to contain in my own small self the infinitude of being. Now I am stillness in the center of the divine whirlwind, a holy dance. There is no end to this for as long as the universe lasts. I recognize it and accept. There are no mistakes. Every moment, every life, is a fragment of the whole—actually a fractal out of which proceeds the wholeness, an eternal galaxy of galaxies unwinding. All I'd considered wounds received in life were simply fragments of the One Being, its infinite colors unwound.

The visages of all the gods, from the most primitive gods of earth to those shimmering in inexpressible light, now appear spiraling one out of the other. From the center of this divine labyrinthine heart, light which is also love pulses, beacons. I hear the Voice, crooning, a Mother-Voice, and am drawn into it as all my questions disappear. "I am Wisdom, the firstborn from Infinity. From me all gods proceed. I am Light from which all worlds arise and Darkness to which they at last return. I am Zoë's dance, the everlasting spiral of Life."

I feel my form, then, merge with Her, and She becomes the path on which I am walking. Around me softly, suddenly, I feel the breeze that flows through the stand of birches in the springtime. I'm on the path through the birches that leads to the center, the mother tree where I sat with Will so long ago. A wren is singing and I walk towards that song. There it is, the tree with ten trunks. I hurry towards it. I've been walking for so long; I'd been more tired than I thought, but now I feel entirely alive.

I reach the tree. I will climb it, I think, as I lift myself up to the nest from which all ten trunks arise, and from that vantage point, with light and music everywhere, I see what looks like someone on the higher branch. Who is it? I focus in. I believe it is...yes....

Light shifts through the branches, and in a long intake of breath I finally recognize what I'd been seeking all this time but had never truly seen before.

COMMON PLACE

Christin Lore Weber

RETURN

AUTUMN AGAIN and the leaves are falling in the birch woods at the edge of what was Will and Bee's alfalfa field. Now and then the locals hear gunshots or are shooting the guns themselves. They'll be bringing home the partridge and grouse for the wives to fix up in a savory gravy stew. Besides the locals, though, are hunters from Fargo, Moorhead, Grand Forks and even as far distant as Minneapolis, because bird hunting around Common Place is said to be the best in the upper Midwest.

Birdie and Karyn each are awakened by the familiar sound, put on their robes, and go to their respective kitchens to put coffee on to brew. Zoë wakes and babbles for a while before she climbs out of her new toddler bed and goes to find her mother. Birdie pours orange juice for her kids and sets it on the table before she fills a mug with coffee for herself. Bud's hunting and left the house while it still was dark. In their Greenleaf homes Mathilde and Marnie don't hear the guns but rise at an early hour anyway because it is their custom. Soon their coffee is brewing as well. Marnie takes a short shower while it brews because she needs to hurry every morning to get to the clinic on time.

Almost simultaneously the four women in their separate homes complete their pre-coffee tasks and go outside to pick up the newspaper. Karyn is slowest because Zoë is holding onto her robe for balance. At more or less the same time, Karyn being last because she needs to strap Zoe into her highchair, the women sit at their respective tables and unfold the paper to read the local news. The same article catches the attention of all of them.

The Prairie Region

News from Greenleaf, Common Place, and Surrounding Townships

October 26, 1978

FARGO HUNTERS FIND BODY

Two Fargo men who were bird hunting on Saturday in a wooded area near Common Place stumbled across the decomposed body of a woman in a cluster of birch trees. The body was determined by authorities to be that of Beatrice Fenelon who disappeared last year following the suicide death of her husband, William Fenelon. Autopsy results indicate the cause of death was a massive cerebral hemorrhage.

Both Beatrice and Will Fenelon grew up in Common Place Township and attended high school in Greenleaf. They married soon after graduation and farmed the land that Beatrice inherited from her parents. Beatrice is survived by her mother, Rose Breault, who is a resident of the State of North Dakota Hospital in Jamestown.

THE END

Widow's Walk

Christin Lore Weber

COVER ARTIST: SHILOH SOPHIA
I HAVE ALWAYS BEEN WITH YOU

This painting was created as a teaching painting over a year long journey with over a 100 women in a sisterhood called Red Madonna. Our theme was to explore the idea of the Queen of the Cosmos—who is she and what does she mean for us today. As the teacher of this course, my painting has many things in it that I am demonstrating, and so lots of details I might not create if I were painting just for myself. However, there is a collective energy of the group. When I paint using Intentional Creativity I don't dominate the process, the paintings turn out however they want, and she had this fierce fire side and I wasn't allowed to touch it or make it more gentle. She is a woman between worlds. Her scroll is her story, the hidden story of the feminine with stardust pouring out. Her heart is her tree of life—an offering, with a green seed within it. Both the challenge and the triumph. She is my Mother Mary as Queen of the Cosmos—doing her work between heaven and earth.

290

The roses are the earth. The names of over 100 women are coded into the painting. This painting is a prayer.

Shiloh Sophia lives life as a great adventure! A renaissance woman who communicates her philosophy through paintings, poetry, teachings and entrepreneurship. For 25 years she has dedicated her soul work to the study and practice of creativity as a path of healing which provides access to consciousness. As a curator and gallery owner, she has represented her own work, as well as that of hundreds of women artists. By the age of 40 she achieved incredible success through being in the top ten percent of sales for contemporary artists in the U.S. Her prolific intuitive painting process led to a desire to teach and provided the foundation for the groundbreaking work on how Intentional Creativity® can give voice to the soul. Her method of 'creating with mindfulness' has reached tens of thousands of students who have gained insight into the hidden self.

Her work is taught widely, at the University in MA and PhD programs, the United Nations CSW, and by hundreds of Certified Teachers and Coaches. At the core of her work is a belief that the right to self express is one of the most basic human rights—"We have a right to know how to access what we think, feel, believe and to express it in our lives." Her life path is a spiritual practice, and an offering that was awakened with the feminine Divine. Her research dives into the

Christin Lore Weber

exploration of the right/left brain connection with the heart and re-inventing personal archetypes as gateways to liberation. "When we find freedom from the trauma of our stories, we can invent our own legends, and do the sacred work of organizing our consciousness."

She is the creator of seven books, as well as a community leader. Having been trained by her mother Caron McCloud the poet, and Sue Hoya Sellars the artist, she brought her gifts of language and image into form through founding the Intentional Creativity® Guild, Cosmic Cowgirls®, Power Creatives TV and Color of Woman®.

THE AUTHOR: CHRISTIN LORE WEBER

Writing a novel is, for me, the work of entering the depth of human reality, an exploration that will take me as far as I am capable into the truth, goodness and beauty of Being itself. It is the art of giving flesh to the Divine Word. It is a contemplative act of peeling away the masks behind which we ordinarily live and coming into contact with the human core that mirrors the Divine. This novel, WIDOW'S WALK, results from my own choice to enter as fully as possible into the secrets of my own widowhood. I am twice a widow, and now married to my third beloved husband. But the mark of the widow is always upon me. Once I arrived at the personal and cosmic emptiness—one of the widow's secrets or sacred mysteries—this story spiraled out from a place well beyond my own personal experience. It captured me and brought me through into an unexpected source of wisdom.

Christin Lore Weber

Christin Lore Weber writes from Casa Chiara Hermitage in the Siskiyou/Applegate Mountains of southern Oregon where she lives a contemplative life with her husband, author John R. Sack. Her early inspiration came from the north of Minnesota where she could be found sitting on a small hillock gazing out at the Rainy River to where it emptied into Lake of the Woods. The only child at her family's fishing lodge, she began early to see beyond the surface of this world. At 17 she left home for life in a Catholic Convent where she spent fourteen years. There she served as a teacher of English, drama, and religion; a counselor; and a director of religious education. She left formal teaching in 1974 to become the chaplain at a treatment center for troubled children. In 1982 she joined Reverend Alla René Bozarth as a co-director of Wisdom House in St. Paul, MN. During these years she earned academic degrees in the humanities, a M.A. in theology, and a Doctorate of Ministry in religion and psychology. Her doctoral dissertation became her first published book.

When her first husband died in 1985 she began to write full time. She had entered early into the community of women attempting to find their way through a theology in mainstream Christian religions that had been written by and for men. In 1986 her book about this exploration, WOMANCHRIST, was accepted for publication by Harper SanFrancisco. From that time forward she has written twelve published books in a variety of genres. WIDOW'S

294

WALK is her thirteenth title. Her work has been published by Harper/Collins, Scribner, Simon&Schuster, Yes International Publishers, and small presses including Loyola University Press, Innisfree Press and Luramedia Press. In recent years she has developed a preference for Independent Publishing which gives her more leeway to be creative.

Christin's association with Shiloh Sophia began in 1995 when Shiloh's early work was just being noticed and Christin had just begun to write her first published novel, ALTAR MUSIC. They became not only colleagues, but beloved friends.

GRATITUDE...

is extended lovingly to all who supported and encouraged me during the writing of this novel.

~To my first two husbands whose deaths set me forth on a journey of inner discovery that has lasted 33 years.

~To my always present husband, John R. Sack, who gives space and time and love and humor and a transcendent heart in support of what I most truly am.

~To Kathleen Jesme, who always tells me the truth with clarity and encouragement.

~To Bill Cunningham, who has agreed to read and comment on every book I've ever written, and whose point of view has become indispensible to me.

~To Sally Benton, who never fails to press deeper into the meanings.

~To Sheri Reynolds, whose keen observations about the writing life and life itself have made up an almost daily correspondence over just shy of thirty years.

~To Hope Robertson, who laughed. But besides that, she held what I'd tried to communicate up to the scrutiny of the most mystical of experiences.

~To Krista May Karels, who so candidly described her experience of labor and birthing.

~To Ní Aódagain, for her encouragement from first line to the last, for her keen writer's eye and her open heart.

~To the Applegate Poet's Association, the first to hear some of this book which I passed off as prose poetry at a workshop with them. They buoyed me up, saying they didn't mind not understanding what I might be doing, they were intrigued. Keep going, they urged, and I did.

~And to Shiloh, who found threads of herself concealed among the sentences.

I am grateful to artists, poets, philosophers, psychologists, physicists and mystics who have entered obliquely into this narrative through their thoughts, rhythms of language, visions. Among them are writers of scriptures, primarily Judeo-Christian and the Gitas. The mystics: Meister Eckhart, Julian of Norwich, Hildegard of Bingen, John of the Cross, and the still living Cynthia Bourgeault for her work concerning the Law of Three. Poet: T.S. Eliot. Priest/Paleontologist Pierre Teilhard de Chardin. The psychoanalyst, Marea Claassen, for accompanying me on this spiraling walk.

The chant honoring Kali came from the *Devi Mahatmya* quoted by Ajit Mookerjee in *Feminine Force*.

Also remembered in the text are *The Divine Comedy* by Dante Alighieri, *The Prophet,* by Kahlil Gibran, and the Catholic liturgy for the Easter Vigil.

I am grateful for earth's places and the people of those places that flowed into this story's descriptions:

Christin Lore Weber

Baudette, Minnesota—the small town of my childhood. Ruch, Oregon and its Community Bible Church. The midlands of Minnesota and North Dakota where I spent many years living and teaching as a Sister of St. Joseph. The Pacific Coast and the mountains of the Applegate in Oregon which combined to create the environment for the stranger's house. I gazed out at those mountains and often at the ocean off the beaches at Brookings or Bandon by the Sea as I listened in my soul for the next groupings of words.

And I do not forget you, the reader, who sat across from me in this room throughout my writing of this story and to whom each word was offered.

www.ingramcontent.com/pod-product-compliance
Lightning Source LLC
Chambersburg PA
CBHW061517020726
47502CB00006B/2107